CRUSHING ON THE PLUG NEXT DOOR 2: FINALE

LAKIA

Crushing On The Plug Next Door 2: Finale
Copyright © 2023 by Lakia
All rights reserved.
Published in the United States of America.
All rights reserved. No part of this publication may be reproduced, distributed, or transmitted in any form or by any means, including photocopying, recording, or other electronic or mechanical methods, without the prior written permission of the publisher, except in the case of brief quotations embodied in critical reviews and certain other noncommercial uses permitted by copyright law. For permission requests, please contact: www.authorlakia.com.
This is a work of fiction. Names, characters, places, and incidents either are the products of the author's imagination or are used fictitiously. Any resemblance of actual persons, living or dead, businesses, companies, events, or locales is entirely coincidental.
The publisher does not have any control and does not assume any responsibility for author or third-party websites or their content.
The unauthorized reproduction or distribution of this copyrighted work is a crime punishable by law. No part of the book may be scanned, uploaded to, or downloaded from file sharing sites, or distributed in any other way via the Internet or any other means, electronic, or print, without the publisher's permission. Criminal copyright infringement, including infringement without monetary gain, is investigated by the FBI and is punishable by up to five years in federal prison and a fine of $250,000 (www.fbi.gov/ipr/).
This book is licensed for your personal enjoyment only. Thank you for respecting the author's work.
Published by Lakia Presents, LLC.

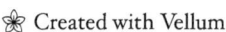 Created with Vellum

JOIN AUTHOR LAKIA'S MAILING LIST!

To stay up to date on new releases, contests, and sneak peeks join my mailing list. Subscribers will enjoy the FIRST look at all content from Author Lakia plus exclusive short stories!

https://bit.ly/2RTP3EV

Alejandro "Dro" King

I've always been a man who wasn't fearful of a motha fucking thing. After all of the shit I've been through and done in life, there was no room for fear. However, hearing that car crash then Yola's weak attempt at a struggle, I was absolutely *petrified*. If I'm being honest, the overwhelming flood of emotions damn near left me paralyzed but I snapped out of that shit and those emotions morphed into rage.

"Baby, what do they look like? Who is trying to take y'all?" I fretted, praying that she could tell me something. The only reason I wasn't on the move was because I didn't know where the hell they were at. Grabbing my gun and keys from the nightstand, I walked out of the bedroom headed for the door to find the girls.

"We will be in touch with our demands. Sit tight." The unfamiliar voice hissed at me before disconnecting the call.

"I'mma kill you!" I roared into the phone although I already knew he couldn't hear me. The overwhelming sense of *terror* that took over me a few moments prior morphed into a rage. I didn't know where they were but I knew I had to get to them. I couldn't live with this type of shit on my conscience, Yola is my woman and I was supposed to be her protector.

"What the fuck is going on?" Xan questioned, stumbling out of Anya's bedroom as I shot the 911 text to Vinny, instructing him to round up the rest of the soldiers and hunt for Ross. That was the only nigga that I could think of at that moment.

"I was on the phone with Yola when somebody crashed into their car. Somebody fucking **snatched** them. I don't know who the fuck it could be because I haven't been into no beef shit besides running into

Ross the other night, but I know they were leaving the club so I already shot off the 911 text and I'm about to see if I can run into the crash site."

"What the fuck man? I bit my tongue for a long time but I don't understand yo dumb ass! You had the chance to go out here and be whatever the fuck you wanted to be but you chose this bullshit and look where it got pops and how that affected us. Now look where it got the women we care about! You're a selfish motha fucka and I find myself in these fucked up positions because of you. Burning down my house, calling me to the stash house earlier because you couldn't get in touch with Yola, but you also couldn't leave until the money was right so you put my freedom in jeopardy. Sadly, that's just the bullshit from the last couple of months but I can keep going," Xan ranted.

My hands were on the doorknob and I was about to exit the home but I had to turn around and address that bullshit. I loved my brother but his ass was out of pocket. At this moment, he should've been ready to ride and help me find them but the nigga chose this crisis to get some shit off his chest.

"See that's where you are wrong. *You* had the world at your feet when you turned eighteen. *I* didn't have a motha fuckin' thing. The narrative that I used my inheritance money to become the plug is some bullshit Priscilla told Big Xan and we know he always believes that bitch so I didn't say shit. While Mama Nadia held onto your money like she was supposed to until you turned eighteen, my mama found a lawyer to help her access my money two years after pops went to prison. She spent that money on coke, partying, and traveling while I was home fending for myself. I couldn't go to college! That bitch told me the best she could do was connect me with my Uncle Macario in Mexico and he would front me enough bricks to help me become the plug. Ever since Maceo died, I been wanting out of this shit, why the fuck you think I opened up Kings and have been scouting other business ventures for me to dump money into?" As I ranted I spotted the sympathy that washed over Xan's face but that shit only further pissed me off. "Ion need your fuckin' sympathy either! You said that shit now stand on it. Pops was dumb as fuck for leaving my money to a bitch he knew wouldn't take care of it. Now you gone help me find the girls or I'mma do it by my motha fuckin' self? Ion have time to hash out this family bullshit right now."

"I'm riding," Xan nodded and we were out the door like ain't shit happen. Throughout our life, that's how we handled a lot of our disputes and the situation was dead to me after that conversation. The nigga could think whatever the fuck he wanted to think after that.

Speeding towards Ybor, the car was silent until I received a call from Vinny. I really ain't like talking business on the phone because that's how my pops got caught up but I'd gladly do prison time if it resulted in me getting Yola and Anya back safely.

"You found him?" I answered the phone on speaker so I could focus on driving.

"Ion think that it was Ross, we found him at Candace's house and he was knocked out cold. They swear he was in the crib all night. I still got him in the trunk but do you really think Ross got that type of pull for some shit like that? When we cut him out, he fell off, po hustlin' and putting on for the hoes, he don't really have the type of money or resources to pull this type of shit off unless he did it himself."

"Take his ass in while I think," I grumbled before disconnecting the call. Using the built up aggression inside of me, I beat on the steering wheel while speeding through another red light.

"Shit, it could've been the Russo family," Xan confessed.

"Who the fuck is that?"

"Remember the Italian mufuckas that came to my office on that bullshit and you pulled up?"

"Yeah, the day yo ass was happy to have the plug for a brother. The nigga that's gone pull up a hunnid deep when issa issue. I remember that shit." I couldn't help myself, I had to point out that this shit wasn't all bad.

"They were mad because dad referred them to me to represent Walter Russo. He's the one who doctors on the Italian mob's people on the street. After meeting with Walter at dad's request, he swore he was innocent of the charges so I told him I would take the case but when I reviewed that evidence, I couldn't stomach that shit. He was producing kiddie porn and starring in the shit. That nigga is exactly where he needs to be and they pulled up on me because they didn't want another lawyer on the case."

"I'm selfish and you just fucking dumb. I know who Walter Russo is but you ain't tell me that's what the fuck the situation was about," I darted my eyes at Xan but refocused on the road because I spotted Yola's Lexus RX surrounded by onlookers and paramedics.

I parked as close as we could and hopped out. When I spotted Anya laying on a stretcher getting checked out by the EMTs, I silently celebrated that my assumptions were wrong and that they didn't take both of the girls. Tears streamed down Anya's face and her eyes lit up once she saw me and Xan approaching.

"Xan!" Anya cried out for him with her arms extended in his direction.

"Do you two gentlemen know Ms. Martin?"

"Yeah."

"Great, she is going to be transported to the hospital but Ms. Martin is clearly drunk and hadn't uttered a word until you guys arrived. I'm not sure if she can formulate a coherent statement at this point. Do you know who was driving? It looks like the driver fled the scene, probably because they were intoxicated as well."

"No, we don't know who was driving," I immediately answered.

If them mob motha fuckas had Yola, the last thing I needed was the cops in my way. They wouldn't think twice about getting rid of her if I got the police involved. Plus I just didn't trust them crooked motha fuckas, I'd rather figure the shit out myself.

"The car is registered to a Yolanda Young..."

"We don't know about anything. I just need to check on my girl," Xan cut him off and walked over to Anya and embraced her in a brief hug. I watched as she cried uncontrollably on the stretcher and prayed that Xan told her to keep her mouth shut. It was a blessing that she wasn't kidnapped as well. Now that she was here to give us information, I needed that shit to come to me and not the cops. Being the plug for the central Florida area was some shit, apparently being a lawyer wasn't safe either. As that thought ran across my mind, I wondered if it was the Italian niggas, why would they take Yola instead of Anya? A lot of shit wasn't adding up but I didn't give a fuck. I wasn't leaving shit to chance.

Priscilla King

"Helllllllllp! Please, somebody helllllllllp!" Gently massaging my temples, I was already agitated as hell and this little bitch was making matters worse. Alejandro had some nerve and I was about to teach his ass a lesson. I brought him into this world and introduced him to the drug game and if he wanted to keep fucking around, I could fuck up the bullshit that he was building. If it wasn't for me, Alejandro wouldn't have had the connections to flourish and become the plug. As far as I'm concerned, Alejandro owed me for pushing him out of my pussy and getting my brother to front him a few bricks. I lost my slim figure and had a hernia all because of my pregnancy with him but he thought he could just cut me off? Nah, Alejandro had another thing coming.

My phone buzzed on the nightstand, and my eyes darted in its direction as my breathing hitched. I sighed in relief when I saw that it wasn't Alejandro calling. As much shit as I was just thinking, I still wasn't prepared to face my son just yet. I had to get myself together before I made my demands. Snatching his little girlfriend wasn't a part of my plans for the evening but it was a spur of the moment decision. She stood her pretty smug ass there questioning me about my son, calling Alejandro that dumb ass nickname that I hated. I named him Alejandro so that's what I wanted people to call him. When Alejandro jumped into the drug game he started with that dumb ass street name and I still wasn't prepared to accept it all these years later.

Snatching the phone off of the counter, I quickly stepped outside to answer the call before the ringing stopped. In the middle of the operator speaking, I pressed **o** to accept the call. "Hello."

"Wassup baby? How you doing? Getting your Monday started on a positive note I hope," Big Xan's gruff voice greeted me.

"Yes, my morning is off to an amazing start," I cooed into the phone.

Every time I spoke with my husband I felt my heart melt. Big Xan was the love of my life and this was our daily routine. He called me every morning when he got up and every evening before he went to bed. When Big Xan couldn't call, he emailed me. Initially, that wasn't the case because Big Xan was housed in a strict facility that barely gave him phone privileges. During that time, I had a lot more freedom to do whatever the fuck I wanted to do without raising suspicions. Even behind those walls Big Xan was extremely positive, I wished that some of that shit would rub off on me because things were gloomy these days. It was getting harder and harder to remain married to him.

I believe that me and Big Xan knew everything about each other except for the one secret that I kept from him, my addiction to cocaine. When me and Big Xan initiated our relationship, he was married to Nadia so it was easy to hide the fact that I used coke as a party drug because he was trying to juggle both relationships in secret. Then when Big Xan left Nadia and married me, things changed.

We had to care for Alexander on the weekends then I couldn't be so free with my shit and that's why I had to leave his ass at home alone. Alejandro was only four years old while Alexander was seven years old. Alexander was old enough to articulate himself clearly, plus the lil boy was smart as hell, I couldn't have him reporting back what he saw when we hung out. If he did, I was sure that Big Xan would've left my ass and took Alejandro away from me. In my young mind, it was better to leave Alexander at home and risk Big Xan finding that out then discovering my drug habit.

Zack stepped outside behind me and placed a gentle kiss on my neck while wrapping his arm around my waist. I instantly rolled my eyes and stepped out of Zack's embrace because I hated this game he played. It was like he had a spidey sense for when Big Xan called because he suddenly wanted to be up under me. Big Xan had been locked up for fifteen years and our vows didn't mean shit to me the moment that judge banged on that gavel and gave him twenty years. I still had to live life for me. Big Xan knew I was a sexual being when we met and that didn't change just because he caught a twenty year sentence. When Big Xan was locked up, I was an exuberant twenty-seven year old, living the lavish life of a hustla's wife, I still had a slew of experiences and destinations on my bucket list.

The first few years, I survived off of Big Xan's money that was stashed away but that soon dried up because I didn't have money coming in but there was definitely money going out. Since my brother knew about my drug addiction he wouldn't front a fucking nickel unless I was clean. This led to me pulling Alejandro's money out early, I had to do what I had to do to survive and maintain my lifestyle.

When Alejandro turned eighteen, I laid out the rules and made things clear. He had to fill in his father's shoes and take care of us. That plan was actually working better than I could've imagined because Alejandro entered the game and capitalized off of that shit better than his father ever could have. Alejandro wasn't just a name in the game or competition for others, he became the plug and life was exceptional until five years ago when he cut me off and left me to fend for myself.

CRASH!

"What the fuck was that, bae?" Big Xan pried.

"I... I... Let me call you back," I abruptly ended the call and addressed Zack. "You and Edward go check from the inside of the house and I'll run around back."

He nodded his head and we took off in opposite directions. Shaking my head, I thought about the dumb ass statement I made to Big Xan just before disconnecting the call. How in the fuck was I going to call him back? Luckily, I knew how the phone systems worked in the prison. Once the call ended Big Xan had to wait thirty minutes to make another phone call and by then, I'd have this little bitch situated with an award winning excuse on my hands.

Running around the side of the house, I confirmed my suspicions, this girl had burst out the window of the bedroom we locked her in. She was in the middle of putting the comforter over the broken glass so she could jump out when Edward pulled her away from the window from the interior of the home. Rolling my eyes, I made my way back inside to meet the pair of brothers I'd been getting high with for a while now. I was romantically involved with

Zack while Edward was his scrawny brother who was just along for the ride.

"Priscilla, please let me go home. The food you tried to give me this morning is going to kill me faster than you ever could. What the fuck was that bullshit?"

"It was vegan food. I eat very clean," I responded, slightly offended because I thought it was great.

"I'm sorry but being a vegan crackhead is crazy. Baby, you might as well eat all of the animals because them drugs gone do you in before the beef and chicken," she cackled.

I couldn't stand this little bitch and I opened my mouth to make it known. "I don't know how Alejandro was putting up with you and your mouth. Since we made it home you haven't stopped screaming and talking shit. I tried to make this as easy for you as possible but it's clear you can't handle that so..."

"You tried to make this *easy* for me? You could've *fucking killed* me!" She closed her eyes for a moment, clearly trying to reel her anger in. "Dro loves every inch of me and I know he is going to fuck somebody up for my busted lip. That's his second favorite body part to suck on."

My face immediately formed a frown of disgust. I almost wanted to vomit, hearing that from this girl. "How could you be so crass in front of your boyfriend's mother?"

She met my glare with a befuddled expression. "Bitch you kidnapped me, the respectability went out of the window when you put me in that dingy ass truck and pointed that gun at me. Why would you kidnap your son's girlfriend?"

"Alejandro has been ignoring me for the past five years. The only reason I didn't snatch Alexander to get his attention is because I can't stand the sight of him."

"Wow, something is really wrong with you. How could you handle your son like this?"

"So Alejandro still cries about how he had to stay by himself while I traveled abroad for six months. I left him with food, a phone, and taught him how to take the bus anywhere he needed to go."

"Wow, so you did that to your son?" Her face seemed genuinely confused and I realized that I was telling on myself the more I spoke.

"You did that to your son and that doesn't seem like deadbeat behavior to you?"

"You're not a young single mom and I pray you never become one so you never have to understand what I was dealing with."

"I was raised by a *real* young single mom. My dad was murdered when I was a toddler so she received no help at all. Hell, my paternal grandmother wouldn't even take the DNA test so we could utilize survivor benefits. But I can assure you my mom never left me alone for months on end to travel abroad. Plus, Dro claims you're the reason he was shot in the chest, who does that as a mother?"

WAP!

Before I knew it, my hand collided with her face while Edward held onto her arms. He was so damn weak that she tore away from him and Zack had to step in and snatch her ass off of her feet before she could touch me. With every word Yola spoke, my level of agitation grew exponentially. If I didn't get my fix soon I was going to fucking lose it. "Shut the fuck up and mind your business!" My eyes swiveled from the girl's to Zack's. My eyes landed on a diamond tennis bracelet on her wrist and my pupils might as well have turned to dollar signs. Snatching the piece of jewelry from Yola's wrist, I shook my head realizing the amount of money my son was spending on this bitch.

"What the fuck?" She fumed, bucking against Zack's embrace but she was no match for him.

"I'm sure Dro bought this for you anyways."

"No the fuck he didn't and I don't give a fuck that you're Dro's mama. When I get out of these cuffs, I'm whooping your ass!" She yelled as I walked towards the door.

"Tie her to the bed and put something in her mouth to shut her the fuck up," I threw over my shoulder. If she kept with that smart ass mouth she wouldn't make it until Alejandro got here.

Dro

Techs, grenades, and all that shit lined the second row of the Suburban that we sat parked in outside of Frank Russo's ex-wife's home. We already ran up in Frank's spot this morning and there was no sign of him. When Xan and Anya were transported to the hospital, he was able to convince her to allow the police to run with their suspicion that the driver fled to avoid a DUI charge. Anya said she didn't regain consciousness until the paramedics placed her on the stretcher so she couldn't tell us shit about who took Yola anyways.

It was safer for us to get Yola back on our own. Plus those motha fuckas ain't never put forth real efforts to locate our missing black women, that shit wasn't going to change now. In under two hours my people found Frank's ex-wife and daughter. We were sitting outside of the crib ready to wreck shit. It was a little before six o'clock in the morning and still dark outside. Watching the lights go on and off as they moved about in the interior of the home, I thought about the diabolical shit I was about to do to get Yola back. Frank's ten year old daughter was headed to summer camp with her mother but they weren't going to make it there.

"Are you sure you want to snatch a kid, bro?"

"About Yola, I don't give a fuck. Fuck this snotty nose jit and her mama. Women and children were off the table until my woman got snatched. Now everybody is fair game. I would've even snatched his wrinkled ass mama and granny but they already in a pinebox."

The lights switched off in the home and I gave Bear the signal to slow roll towards the house. Pulling my ski mask down, I was ready to jump out and execute our plan. We reached their driveway just as my phone rang. The woman and child stepped out of the house and I signaled for my men to move in without me because it was my mother calling. She called my phone at least once a month for the past five years but I didn't have shit to say to her treacherous ass. However, these were extenuating circumstances and I answered the phone just to make sure that she was safe with all the shit going down around me without real answers.

"Wassup? You straight?" I answered the phone, never tearing my eyes away from the two story modern home in question. My men hopped out, guns drawn, snatching the oblivious pair right out of the driveway.

"I have your little girlfriend and now since you have been hiding from me, forcing me to search high and low for you, now it's your turn to search for me," I could hear my mother's voice trembling through the phone but I knew she wasn't lying. As Priscilla made her announcement, the screaming woman and child were stuffed into my truck as Bear sped away from the curb.

"Stop the car and tell them niggas in the truck behind us to stand down. Tell everybody to stand down!" I ordered before redirecting my attention to the fearful mother-daughter duo in the seat next to me. "April fools in June," I shrugged and leaned over to open the door and allow them to step out of the truck. They both sat there crying and confused, further pissing me off. "Get the fuck out before I change my mind!"

The mother jumped before hopping out of the truck with her daughter's hand gripped tightly into hers. Once they were out, I slammed the door shut, leaving them standing in the middle of the road as Beast sped out of the neighborhood. "You crazy ass bitch, you kidnapped Yola? You think life is a fuckin' game don't you? Where y'all at?"

"Cálmate (calm down), I'm not going to hurt her," she chuckled. "I have been snooping on her social media account for the last few minutes and I see you have her name tattooed on you so it's clear you love her."

"Priscilla, let me get this straight... you almost just got me into a war with the Italian Mob because you wanna play games like this? I was in the process of kidnapping a little girl and her mom because I thought her father had Yola and I can't find him. We had to give Yola's sister Xanax to get her to calm down after we told her what happened and you on my line talkin' 'bout calm down?"

"No, don't put that on me, Alejandro! Your weakness for a piece of pussy almost put you in that situation and when you started in this game, I told you not to allow a woman to enter your heart and become your weakness for your competition to exploit. You better get here quick because the mouth on this bitch is about to push me over the edge and I'm sober so you know it won't take much for that to happen," she spat before disconnecting the phone.

"Take me back to Yola's house!" I roared, punching the shit out of the back of the seat and Beast stepped on the gas. On the drive there I called my mother back to back and this bitch ignored every call.

When we pulled up to the house I sprinted inside and found Anya sitting in the living room with Xan. Her eyes were puffy from crying and she jumped to her feet, searching my eyes for answers. "Did you find her?" Anya faltered.

"Nah, but I know who has her. It's *my mom* so I'm sure that she won't hurt her."

"What the fuck!?" Xan exclaimed, stepping to me.

He knew I was lying but I didn't want to make shit harder for Anya at that moment. Plus I didn't want her running back to tell their moms shit yet. If Priscilla harmed Yola in any way, I'd slit her throat without thinking twice. That shit might sound harsh to say about your mama, but you don't know that bitch. Mama Nadia was there for me during my formative years more than my own mama. Priscilla didn't decide she wanted to be a mother and foster a real bond until I turned eighteen and she introduced me to the game, teaching me almost everything that I knew. I gripped Xan's shirt and pulled him outside before he could say anything to hurt my plans in front of Anya. "Let me holla at Xan real quick. We are going to go get Yola, I just need you to relax, sis in law."

The front door closed once we stepped out and Xan pulled away from me, shoving me hard as fuck in the chest. "I ain't lying to Anya. We don't know what the fuck yo crazy ass mama is capable of. Where the fuck they at?"

"I don't know, she told me to come find her," I exhaled deeply. "You not about to tell Anya shit. If I thought she would hurt Yola, I would be honest about that shit. I *love* that girl, I don't know what the fuck I would do if anything happens to her and I'm definitely not trying to protect my mama over her. Now I need you to quell Anya and pull some strings so we can go see pops in person. My people are already trying to see what they can find out about Priscilla, but I know pops got a line on her."

Xan brushed his hands across his waves then shot me an evil glare before silently retreating to the interior of the home to do what needed to be done. After Anya was comfortable with two of my men at the crib with her, Xan made a few calls and pulled some strings on the legal side for us to visit our father as legal counsel instead of a regular family visit that would've taken time to schedule.

He was housed at a prison in northern Florida but it was six o'clock in the morning and visitation hours were from nine to three so we would definitely make it. Xan drove us to the prison in his Benz with a truck full of my niggas following close behind us. My sleep deprived ass wanted to smoke bad as fuck but Xan would've probably put me out on the side of the interstate if I tried that shit. I spent most of the drive blowing up Priscilla's phone until she must've blocked my ass because the shit wasn't ringing anymore.

Around one o'clock we pulled up to the jail and Xan led us inside where we were searched and led into a private area to meet with pops since we were here in attorney-client capacity. When my dad entered the room, sheer shock and glee spread across his face. We spoke on the phone regularly until I cut Priscilla off five years ago. I still don't know what she told pops but he called me talking too crazy for me. He didn't even realize that I was still recovering from bullet wounds that I received because of *her*. Xan's relationship with our father was always rocky because of our childhood. After greetings and long embraces, we sat at the table and I got right down to it because the clock was steadily ticking and the love of my life was with a woman that I despised.

"How can I find my mama?" I pried.

"Why? The last time I checked, you weren't footing her bills or fucking with her. You ain't have shit good to say about my wife and that's why we've been distant. She was a no good liar and all types of shit."

"Don't sit up here chastising me about *your wife*! Your wife is a powder head bitch who…"

"Aye, watch yo mouth talking about my wife, boy!" He snarled, old ass head whipping in my direction so motha fuckin' fast, I thought it might snap off his shoulders.

"I don't know what type of wool she got pulled over your eyes but you need to open them bitches. You doing a bunch of shit that's not even in your character. The Italians tried to rough Xan up in his office but I got one of my boys working in his office and bought him a nice AK that fits in the bottom drawer of the custom desk so they were straight."

"What does that have to do with my wife?"

"We ain't dumb, we know she had something to do with that shit too. *Your wife* out here snorting powda and doing her, she ain't worried about you. I ain't fucked with her since I was 21. I'm 26, I'll be 27 in a few weeks. That's five going on six whole years. I bet she didn't tell you that. I bet she didn't tell you that she found a lawyer to get my money out of my trust fund before I turned 18. Snorted that shit up and traveled the world with my money. Then when I graduated from high school, she informed me that college wasn't an option because we couldn't afford it. Told me my Uncle Macario would front me a few bricks if I stepped to him correctly and she could help me fill your shoes. She wants me sitting on the bench next to you. Once I started to see shit around me for what it was, I was done with her. I took care of her ass for years then she fucked one of my enemies and tried to set me up when I told her she couldn't get another penny out of me unless she went to rehab."

"Nah, Priscilla wouldn't do anything like that," he refuted. "Even if she did, why would you want to find her all of a sudden if you haven't fucked with her in five years?"

Furious, I pulled my shirt down to expose the two bullet wounds in my chest. "I got these because of my mama, yo powda head wife is a leach who will bleed you dry… she don't care who the fuck you are and I had to accept that about my own mama so you gotta accept that shit about your wife. Now I found the woman that completes me, I love her and would lay it all down for her... and your crazy ass wife rammed into her car to daze her because she couldn't snatch Yola straight up, my bitch a fighter and would've ripped her frail ass apart. While she was dazed, she kidnapped her, then called my phone like this shit was a fucking game." I was breathing hard as fuck now because my level of respect for my father was dwindling with every word. Flashbacks of our childhood when our father didn't believe Xan about Priscilla flooded my mind. After seeing how easy it was for Priscilla to lie to our pops about what Xan said, I knew I didn't stand a chance so my childhood was full of silent bullshit because this nigga didn't listen.

Tears filled my father's eyes but he wouldn't get any sympathy from me and by the look of Xan's cold eyes, he wasn't offering up any either. "She has a cabin in Morriston, Florida."

I jolted from my chair ready to take off after my pops rattled off the address but his words stopped me in my tracks. "If what you said is true..."

"If?" I scoffed because I no longer cared to prove shit to him. "Say less."

Marching out of the small cold room with Xan right behind me, I couldn't give a fuck about anything but determining the travel time from this prison to Morriston. In an effort to keep Xan clean, I was sending his ass home to be with Anya because I had no idea the type of shit that was going to pop off if my mama was at this address in Morriston. Xan drove me to the gas station around the corner where Beast was parked and I climbed into his Suburban to embark on the hour and twenty minute drive to the address in question. We eased into the driveway and I spotted my mother's smug ass sitting in a chair smoking a cigarette.

"You want us to come in with you?" Beast coaxed.

He knew the intimate details of the relationship with my mother. Outside of Maceo, he was the only one who knew everything I dealt with when it came to Priscilla. Up until earlier today, Beast even knew more than Xan. I kept my brother and Mama Nadia in the dark about Priscilla pushing me into the dope game because they had already been there for me in more ways than I could ever thank them for.

"Y'all can step out of the truck but Ion think she's that crazy. I'll go in and grab Yola myself. Y'all watch out for anybody trying to take off."

I stepped out of the truck and Priscilla jumped from her chair with a huge Cheshire grin spread across her face. She sprinted in my direction as if she was about to embrace me in a hug. With my arm extended, I stopped her ass from embracing me. "If you don't take me to wherever you got Yola, I swear to God I'm about to shoot the shit out of you in this driveway," I assured her, pulling my gun from my waist and aiming it in the middle of her forehead. "Vamos! (Let's go!)" I barked, gently nudging the barrel of the gun into her flesh.

The wild look in her eyes let me know that she was high and fear definitely wasn't imminent in her because she immediately started talking shit. "Dro, I didn't hurt her and you are overreacting. I had to do something to get your attention. You act like you don't owe me! If it wasn't for me, you wouldn't have been able to become the plug... this bitch wouldn't even want you if you were broke. You always said you'd never date a gold digging woman like me but you got one that's out and proud about that shit. The last picture she posted with you in it said, and I quote, *since you're in my business this my trick*. What type of bullshit is that, Alejandro?"

"The difference is, Yola has her own money and doesn't need mine. I do what I do for her because I want to, not because I have to. If I disappear tomorrow Yola would still live the same lifestyle without me. Clearly, yo ass can't relate to that because as soon as Big Xan was sent up the road you were broke and had to steal from me to get by."

I snatched her silly ass up by her hair and turned her around to face the house. With the gun nuzzled against her temple, Priscilla led the way towards the cabin. If this were anybody else, we wouldn't have exchanged words, there would've only been bullets flying but this was a delicate situation. Murdering Priscilla would cost me the connection to the purest coke coming into Florida and start a war with my Uncle Macario's Cartel. No matter how much coke she snorted, Priscilla was still the offspring of a Leyva and that meant she was off limits, even to me, her son. With each step we took towards the door my mind raced faster, attempting to think of ways to dead this situation without going to war with my own family.

Alexander "Xan" King Jr.

Speeding down I-75, the conversation between my father and Dro plagued my wandering thoughts. I wanted to express my grievances with Big Xan but now wasn't the time. If something happened to Dro, I'm not sure that I'd ever recover. Anyone who met Anya and Yola could see how tight their bond was and I'm positive that Anya was experiencing those same feelings.

As I pulled into the driveway of Anya and Yola's home, I initiated a call to Raymond, the private investigator that often worked on my cases. He was one of the best in the game and I called him as we drove to the prison to put him on the job of collecting any information that he could on Priscilla over the last five years. Although Dro had a potential address for Priscilla, I still wanted to do whatever I could to bring Yola home safely, my girl's sanity depended on it.

"I was just about to call you," Raymond greeted me.

"What intel could you find on Priscilla?"

"The address that you texted me is in the name of Priscilla King and that's the only property that she has purchased in the last five years. I was able to hack her icloud based off of the phone number she called Dro from and according to her texts, Priscilla facilitated a meeting between Frank Russo and her brother Macario in Mexico three or four months ago."

Gently massaging my temples, I wasn't even surprised to hear that Priscilla had something to do with the Russo family. It made sense now why my dad was probably so adamant about me helping Walter Russo with his case.

"Is there anything else?"

"Not at the moment, I'm still researching but I wanted to give you the information that I have gathered so far."

"Thanks Raymond. Call me immediately if you discover anything else."

"I got you."

We disconnected the call and I stepped out of the car just as Yola's mother and stepfather swerved into the driveway next to me. Everything happened so fast, the front door swung open and Anya stepped outside with three of Dro's men right behind her as Mr. Al rushed me. He was a big cocky nigga, looked like he should've been on somebody's football field playing defensive tackle. I was barely out of the car when he snatched me up by my shirt and pushed me up against my Benz.

The men Dro left behind rushed over in our direction but I held up my hand to stop them before they took it too far. I was sympathetic to their feelings but Mr. Al had me fucked up putting his hands on me. Shoving Mr. Al off of me, Anya scurried between the two of us and I straightened out my shirt.

"I'm going to ask you one question and I need an honest answer. Where the fuck is Yola?"

"Where is she, Xan?" Mrs. Latifah sobbed behind him.

"I don't know for sure yet but Dro is on his way to find her."

"Anya said it was Dro's mother. What type of shit is that? Why would she do that to my baby?"

Mr. Al embraced Mrs. Latifah and my heart crumbled into pieces hearing her inconsolable sobs. My eyes darted to Anya because we agreed not to tell them for the time being. Anya must've read my mind because she started explaining.

"I had to tell her. Yola was supposed to open the shop today and when she didn't show up, the stylists were calling Mrs. Latifah."

"You don't have to explain shit to this nigga. I need you to be explaining why you are here instead of with Dro looking for Yola?" Mr. Al went from addressing Anya to chastising me.

"With all due respect, Ion have to explain my presence to nobody. Now I already let you get off with putting your hands on me but I won't be tolerating the disrespect. If we are going to engage in respectful dialogue then I will inform you that I'm here because I would kill that bitch if I went and that's still Dro's mom so he gotta handle that. Plus I needed to be here to make sure that Anya is straight and to see if my private investigators could find any additional information on Priscilla just in case they aren't at the address that my dad gave us for Priscilla. Dro loves Yola and he is going to do anything within his power to bring her home safely."

"Is Priscilla's last name King like yours and Dro's?" Mr. Al questioned.

"Yeah and her maiden name is Leyva." I slowly nodded my head and he gripped Mrs. Latifah's hand before whispering something in her ear.

"Bet, we are going to conduct our own investigation to see what we can find."

Without another word, they took off and Anya rushed over to wrap her arms around me. I instantly hugged her back and allowed all of her weight to bog my body down. "Have you eaten since we left this morning?"

Anya's bloodshot eyes glanced up to meet mine and she shook her head no. Leaning down, I planted a kiss on her forehead. "Let's take a ride to get something to eat before you pass out on a nigga."

"I can't leave. I'm sure Mrs. Latifah is going to tell my mom everything and then she'll be coming over to get on my ass for not telling them what happened as soon as it went down," Anya sniffled. She was still dressed in the pajama set and black slippers that I left her in earlier. My baby was going through it and Dro needed to come through with some answers ASAP because there ain't no telling what those two went to do. If they chose to go to the police we can't do shit about that now, it's their daughter.

"They will be alright, we did the best thing for the situation. Look at Mr. Al and Mrs. Latifah, running off talking about they are going to conduct their own investigation. I would never mislead you, Dro's mom is a nutty bitch, but I don't think she'd hurt Yola. Now come on, you don't even have to get dressed, you can go as is."

I guided Anya around the car to show her that it wasn't a request but a demand. Anya slid into the passenger seat and I rounded the car as one of Dro's men approached me. "Dro told us to watch over you while he's out of the city."

"Dro ain't my fuckin' daddy and Ion need a babysitter," I shook my head and lifted my shirt to display my gun, secured safely on me. "I'm strapped and my AK is sitting on the backseat. All my shit legal so I'm better off watching myself anyways."

"But..."

I ignored him and climbed into my car, speeding out of the driveway before they could protest further. We stopped at Chick-fil-A on Gandy Boulevard and hit the long ass drive thru line. The entire time we waited for our food I gripped her hand and placed gentle kisses on it sporadically. After securing our food, I continued west on Gandy Boulevard.

"Where are we going?"

"To relax for a minute so you can eat. I know it's easier said than done but I'mma get the job done."

Anya leaned her head back onto the seat as we drove another ten minutes to Gandy Beach. It was nightfall by the time we arrived at the beach, setting the perfect scene for relaxation. I turned the lights off, turned on some classic R&B, and let the windows down so we could enjoy the soothing sounds of the waves washing ashore. Anya was clearly hungry because she wasted no time digging into her nuggets and fries. I don't know why I chose Chick-fil-A because now my pescatarian ass was sitting here eating nothing but fries and sipping on a Sprite.

After we finished eating I pulled her feet into my lap and gently massaged them. I noticed that she always stuck with the classic white toes and that shit always looked amazing on her perfect little feet. Her phone rang and she looked down with an apprehensive expression on her face.

"What's wrong?" I questioned.

"It's Yola's friends that came to town for the grand opening. They are texting asking if everything is okay because they haven't been able to get in touch with Yola."

"Just tell them that she is really sick or something and she will call them when she is feeling better."

Anya took a moment and clicked around on her phone before

sliding it onto the dashboard. "No matter how grown we are, Chick-fil-A will always remind me of the times when me and Yola used to skip school. That was always our go to lunch. I remember we got caught by Mr. Al, eating Chick-fil-A in the mall skipping school after winter break. They took both of our cars for the rest of the year and made us ride the bus to school," she laughed. "That shit was so ghetto. We were used to alternating days that we would drive each other to school and we always stopped for McDonald's breakfast. All that was gone in the blink of an eye."

"Yeah, I was a geeky lil nigga in high school, I never skipped school. My ass stayed in them books and class. My favorite show was *Law & Order* growing up, then when my father went to prison, I was intrigued by the criminal justice system and knew I wanted to be a criminal defense attorney. In my young mind, I used to say that I was going to go to law school to get my dad out of prison. I did research his case for a while but the older I got, the less I had contact with my father. Even behind those walls, you can't tell him shit and he doesn't listen to anything you say. I hired another attorney for him and he is also a beast in the courtroom too."

"Well I hope that you guys get back on the right track soon," she took a deep breath. "I actually admire the fact that you knew exactly what you wanted to be and went out there to do it. When I went to college, I thought that I wanted to be a nurse but I quickly learned that I had a weak stomach so I decided to switch my major to business. When I graduated from college, I ended up saying fuck that degree and following my dreams of becoming an interior designer and here I am. Still hustling and working towards my goal of becoming a household name."

"I admire you for making your own decisions and walking your own path in life. That's really all that matters."

"Yeah. Let's get out, I just want to breathe in some of the night air for a minute."

Complying with her request, we took our shoes off and exited the car. We allowed our barefeet to sink into the sand as we searched for the perfect spot to observe the tranquil scene. I wrapped my arms around Anya from behind as we stared out into the dark waters. The amount of tension I felt in Anya's body wasn't surprising, I would be the same way if it was Dro. "He's going to bring Yola home," I assured her, planting a kiss on top of her head as I held her tighter.

Yolanda "Yola" Young

𝒜s tough as I was acting in the presence of Priscilla, I'm not afraid to admit that I was terrified for real. Although I wasn't positive what type of beef shit Dro and his mama had going on, my critical thinking skills allowed me to draw a few conclusions. Hell, sitting tied to this bed like a prisoner for real, I had nothing but time to think and let my brain run wild. After Priscilla snatched my bracelet, she left me and these tall ass strange men alone in the cabin for an hour or two. Their creepy asses took turns watching over me the entire time Priscilla was gone. When she returned they all left me alone for a few minutes. I spent that short amount of time struggling against the ropes that bound me to the old ass oakwood bed.

When the tall healthy looking one returned to the room, it was clear that he was high as hell. Dro previously mentioned that his mother did coke but the way that he was nodding off, they clearly elevated to harder drugs. If functioning junkies had a face, it would be these two because I never would've assumed that was the case upon initially seeing them. Unfortunately, the scrawny dude couldn't pass the junkie sight test. I took one glance at him when we entered the cabin last night and knew he was on that shit. This revelation further increased my anxiety in this situation because junkies were liable to take shit to great lengths to accomplish their goals.

"Vamos!" That loud voice coming from outside startled me for a millisecond then a smile spread across my face. I knew that voice, whether it was joyful, furious, or melancholy, Dro's voice would always stand out to me.

The healthy looking junky shot up out of his seat in the rocking chair across from me and said something in Spanish, suddenly the tall scrawny one entered the room and stood next to me. The door was wide open so I could see the healthy one march down the hallway and peek out of the blinds in the living room before running in the opposite direction and jolting out of the backdoor. I was confused as fuck but didn't have time to wonder what the fuck he had going on because I heard voices approaching the front door. My ears were burning to hear whatever Dro and Priscilla were discussing. If it was anyone else, I knew for sure that Dro would've shot this shit up. He didn't talk about his business with me but I knew who the fuck I was dealing with, I'm not obtuse. I couldn't make out the conversation until the door came open.

"Ion wanna hear shit you gotta fucking say because you ain't getting a fuckin' dime out of me. The only reason you ain't sinking to the bottom of some river connected to a bunch of cinder blocks is because you're my mother and have a connection to the Leyva Cartel but you're wearing me thin as fuck Priscilla! Got me ready to say fuck it, let's start a war."

"**Don't** call me Priscilla, I'm your mother!"

"Dro!" I screamed out. "I'm back here!"

Our eyes connected as I sat on the bed with my hands tied to the headboard. His freckled face wore the ugliest scowl I'd ever witnessed. I'm sure the scrawny man standing next to the bed noticed too because he was trembling.

"We need a hundred grand if you want us to release her!" Priscilla exclaimed.

Dro shoved his mother out of the way and her slim frame tumbled to the ground. She was already high and unsteady on her feet so I'm sure he didn't use much force to cause her to tumble over. Dro lifted his gun, aimed it at the scrawny dude who was helping Priscilla. I closed my eyes as the scrawny man attempted to run because I didn't want to see what was coming next. Dro pulled the trigger and I heard his body plop down in the middle of the room.

"Keep your eyes closed, bae," Dro requested and I did. I felt his presence when he dropped down next to me. Dro pulled out a pocket knife and cut me loose before carrying me out of the room and placing me back on my feet. He tried to hug me but I had other immediate plans.

LAKIA

Pulling away from Dro's embrace, I charged Priscilla and rained blows to her smug face. This hoe had so much shit to say when she had a gun in her hand and two men by her side to hold me back. I still felt the stinging sensation from her slapping me hours ago and I'm positive my lip looked a fucking mess because it felt big as hell. She fell to the ground and I was on her ass, left right left, straight face shots. Priscilla's high ass put up a little fight too, scratching my neck while she flailed below me, attempting to get me off of her. When Dro snatched me off of Priscilla, I was breathing heavily and still trying to free myself from his grasp so I could tag that ass a little more. Priscilla was still breathing so I wasn't satisfied. I'd never felt more vulnerable and violated than I did since she put me in the back of that stank ass truck and brought me here at gunpoint. Yet she was telling Dro that it wasn't a big deal.

"I'm a big deal bitch! This entire situation is a big deal! I mean something to somebody! Hell, I mean something to a lot of people!" I screamed across his shoulder as tears streamed down my face.

"It's over, baby," Dro whispered in my ear and gently rubbed his hands up and down my back as I caved and expelled my feelings through tears and loud sobs. "Nobody will ever hurt you again, you hear me?" I nodded my head yes although I didn't believe that shit. "Priscilla, if you love me and want to make it out of this situation alive, you'll go to rehab. If not, you, a few cinder blocks, and the ocean floor can get real acquainted and I'll have to deal with the consequences as they come."

"You are going to let them get away with this?" I snatched away from Dro and glared into his eyes, fury filling my soul with each breath I took.

"It ain't that simple Yola, trust me. I know it's fucked up but she still has some pull that I can't explain to you right now," Dro sympathetically explained before refocusing his attention on Priscilla, holding her jaw in the middle of the floor. I trusted Dro and looking at Priscilla, I felt sympathy because drugs could do a number on one's mental so a sober mind probably wouldn't have pulled the crackhead shit she did. "But let me make this clear, if you don't get clean and if you ever contact me, Yola, or anybody associated with us, I won't hesitate to kill you my fuckin' self. This is going to be my wife one day and..."

"You wanna marry me?" I blushed, smiling with a fat ass lip.

"Man Yola, I was about to kidnap one of them Italian mob nigga's daughter and baby mama because I thought they had you. It was about to be a war and I didn't give a fuck. About you, everybody was getting laid down." This crazy nigga knew how to get my panties wet. I leaned up and planted my swollen lips on his for a brief peck. "So what's it going to be Priscilla? Rehab or hell?"

"Fine, I'll go to rehab," she sat up in the middle of the floor and folded her arms across her chest like a pouting toddler. Shaking my head, my wild spoiled ass didn't have shit on this bitch.

The sound of an engine revving caught our attention and the sound of a dirt bike taking off followed immediately after. Shots rang out in the yard and I figured it was the tall man driving off. Dro ran towards the door and I was right on his heels. There were two black SUV's parked in the driveway and one peeled off, chasing the man on the dirt bike.

"Who the fuck was that?" Dro turned around from his spot on the porch to question Priscilla but she was laid in the middle of the floor, looking at the ceiling. That fast, she secured a needle and drugs and was administering the potent substance intravenously. A bright smile spread across her beautiful face as she pulled the needle out.

"I don't know who that was but I just needed one more high before you make me go to rehab," she slurred.

"Shit! She playing with needles now?" Beast questioned, approaching the door with his eyes trained on Priscilla.

"That's why she did this dumb ass shit. We gone check her ass into rehab then go home," Dro explained. "Did they say they caught whoever drove off on the dirt bike?"

"Nah, they said he ducked off in some woods on the dirt bike and they couldn't make it that deep in there driving the truck. They are coming back now."

"How many people helped Priscilla and did you hear her say their names?"

"It was just the dead man in the back and another man about the same height, he just had a little more weight on him. They looked like they could be brothers but I'm not sure if they really were. I didn't see anyone else here, the one who got away ran off as soon as he saw you through the window," I confessed.

Anguish, frustration, and resentment washed across Dro's face simultaneously as he caught another glimpse of Priscilla, high and happy as fuck. She didn't give a single fuck about the turmoil she was causing in her son's life. I felt terrible for him, I couldn't imagine the various emotions that he was struggling with at that moment. Despising your mother for all of the harm she's done to you throughout your life while still having love for her because she's your mother.

Earlier, when Priscilla mentioned leaving Dro at home alone, I was completely shocked. I had no idea that his mother handled him like that as a child. Gently gripping Dro's hand, I squeezed it to let him know that I was here with him. The sound of the other truck returning forced Dro to finally move his feet and speak again. "Me and Yola are driving home solo. Get that body cleaned up in that back room and then y'all get her back to the city until I can have Pinky secure a spot in a rehab facility for her."

"How are we all going to fit in the truck with her?" One of the men wondered aloud.

"Shit, ride in the trunk, lap up, catch an Uber? Ion give a fuck," Dro gritted before pulling me towards the other truck. Once we were securely inside, I spotted Beast carrying Priscilla out of the house. She gently ran her hand along his jawline and he swatted her hand away.

Dro started the truck and backed out of the driveway. "I apologize about everything. Are you okay? Do you think we should go to the hospital before we drive home? I didn't even have a chance to ask before you started beating her ass in there." Dro chuckled softly but it wasn't his usual arrogant laugh.

"I'm fine, I've been alert as hell since they put me in that dingy ass truck." I detailed.

"Dingy ass truck? Do you remember the make, model, or color? We didn't see any vehicles when we pulled up at the cabin and I still need to find out who helped Priscilla. I might not be able to knock her head off but that nigga is dead, I don't give a fuck who it was."

"We drove here in a black Dodge Ram with a red logo on the side. I know that you are going to handle the situation but baby, are you okay?"

"Priscilla is Priscilla, always going to be who she is. I do hate to see it come to this."

"I'm going to be here for you every step of the way."

"That's why I love you," Dro expressed before leaning over to plant a kiss on my cheek.

"I love you too," I cooed.

"Let me call Xan and let him know that I found you so Anya isn't worrying herself to death at home."

"With everything happening so fast, I forgot Anya was in the car with me when the accident happened. How is she?"

"She's good, they cleared her to leave the hospital after running a few tests. No concussion or anything."

"Thank God!" I exhaled.

We spent the next few minutes on the phone with Anya and my mom, ensuring them that I was doing just fine. My mom wanted to see me immediately because Mr. Al had already used his connections in the police department to get them information on Priscilla. The ride was silent once they were off the phone and Dro looked over at me with a big grin on his face. This was his first time relaxing his face since he saw me tied up to the bed.

"You wanna go get married?"

"Like right now?" I puzzled.

"Yeah, this shit fucked me up in more ways than one. I want you to be my wife... since I didn't give you a cute proposal, you can pick out whatever ring you want, just slide my card. We can fly to Vegas and get this shit done."

The idea was wild but I knew that I loved Dro and he was the one for me. On the other hand, I wasn't sure if he really meant it right now because we just went through some outlandish shit. His own mother kidnapped me to extort him for drug money. Although Priscilla still kept her appearance up, the poor lady was in such a bad mental state that she didn't even have a solid plan to get money from Dro. Her high ass just nicely requested money when he got there, no guns drawn or anything, as if that was going to work. She flashed her gun at me earlier but they were probably too high to even remember they were in the middle of conducting a kidnapping.

Dro's phone rang and he looked at it for a moment before answering the phone on the car speaker. The automatic message went through its spiel and Dro accepted his father's phone call.

"Hello."

"Hey Dro, how did things work out today?"

"Everything went good. I'm sitting with Yola right now and I hope that this will finally be the thing you need to open your eyes and accept who your wife is. She shot up right in front of me today, she might look good, but them drugs have a bad hold on her. I'm putting her into rehab but I can't make any promises outside of that."

"Damn Priscilla," he sighed in disbelief. "Are you sure that's what you saw?"

"Look, either believe it or don't. Ion give a fuck no more. After this shit, I'm not dealing with her *ever* again and she better stay the fuck away from me and mine even if she does get clean. There are plenty of other bitches out here dating prisoners, you could've been secured yourself a new shorty but you wasting your time on a crackhead bitch that don't give a fuck about none of us. I gotta go before you piss me off even more and I slip up and say some shit to incriminate myself."

Dro hung the phone up before his father could respond. We continued through traffic and he looked over at me with questioning eyes. This shit was all too much to handle.

"So you don't want to marry a nigga?"

"I do, but I think you're being impulsive. It's clear that you don't fuck with your family like that but I do and I want Mr. Al to walk me down the aisle in my big white dress..."

"A white dress with the way you fuck? Nah shorty, off-white at best," he chuckled to himself.

"Shut up boy," I gently nudged his head, happy as hell to see his humor coming back to him. "I don't care how much of a hoe I was in my past life, I'm wearing a white dress. So like I was saying, wedding dress, aisle, my family, and your brother and we can get married. Deal?"

"Bet," he squeezed my hand and I leaned over to plant a kiss on his cheek.

"You was trying to have me with this fat ass lip in my wedding pictures," I expressed, pulling the mirror down to check my appearance.

"Shit, them lips seem just fine to me. Look like they ready to slob all on this dick for your hardheaded ass not coming home last night and doing a music video with that nigga Tazz. It's his lucky day because I was gone spin that nigga's block but I had to come play captain save a hoe."

"Boy fuck you, after all of this trauma you brought into my life, you can call me Pillow Princess Yola because all I'm going to do is lay back and get my pussy ate for a lil while. Oh, and not only do you owe me whatever engagement right I want, your mother stole my tennis bracelet. I'm sure she took that shit to the pawnshop and used it to buy those drugs."

"Nah, I ain't replacing shit another nigga bought you. You already told me one of those niggas bought your jewelry and shit."

"So what! I want my shit replaced Dro," I whined.

"Fuck that bracelet and the nigga that bought it. If you wanna cry about that shit, he can come pick you up."

"Ughhhhhhh! After everything I went through the last few hours, I thought you'd rescue me and be all sweet and shit, but nope, still an asshole."

"You love this asshole and I'mma spend the rest of my life making it up to you."

He pulled my knuckle to his lip and planted a gentle kiss on it as we continued down the interstate.

Anya Martin

Happy tears slid down my face and relief spread through my body once I heard my sister's voice on the phone. Prior to the phone call, Xan kept assuring me that Dro would bring Yola home safely but there was always that sliver of harsh reality that snuck up on me in every situation. When we received the FaceTime call, Xan and I were seated in my living room with my parents, allowing our anxious thoughts to fill the deathly silent room. I was so grateful that Xan forced me to go to the beach earlier because I was starting to feel as if I were suffocating in that house. My parents interrupted our peaceful time at the beach and demanded that I come home because they were worried about me. I don't know, seeing that big ass gun on Xan's back-seat put my mind at ease and made me feel like he would protect me just like he told Dro's bodyguards he would.

"Now that we know for sure that Yola is safe, we will get out of here. I want to go check on Latifah and Al, they were going through it when we spoke to them earlier," my mom announced, standing to embrace me in a firm hug. Mr. Tom, my stepdad did the same and we walked them to their car and watched them leave.

Exhaling deeply, I was so happy that they were gone. I loved my parents, but my mother's fidgety ass was making it harder for me to relax. Dro's men stood around the perimeter of the house and I was ready for them to go too. Xan must've read my mind because he gave them their walking papers too. We retreated to the interior of the home and I went to the cabinet in search of the wine but we were out.

"Do you want to go grab a few drinks and maybe some wings? I need a drink real bad after all of the stress I've endured over the last twenty-four hours."

"I'm down to go anywhere with you as long as you're going to smile.

It's a three hour drive from where Yola and Dro are coming from, we'll probably still beat them home," he explained.

"Let me take Rex outside then I'll get dressed," I informed him.

Two hours later we were at the bar eating lemon pepper chicken wings and I was on my fourth lemon drop. Xan was taking shots of Hennessy and all of our troubles seemed to dissipate.

"It's so crazy how we both have the same exact sibling dynamic. Me and you are the chill, laid back ones and then we have Yola and Dro stressing us out to the fucking max every chance they get," I rambled.

"Definitely, but I'm used to the shit. I wouldn't trade Dro for the world."

"I wouldn't trade Yola either. Thinking about losing her today had all types of shit going through my mind. It was like I was living but I couldn't breathe until I saw her face on my phone screen."

"Shit, I couldn't breathe either," Xan confirmed before leaning in to plant a kiss on my lips. "We don't have to worry about that though, it's all positive vibes for the rest of the night."

Xan pulled out his phone and I watched patiently as he clicked around on his phone. "Is it Dro texting you?"

"Nah, the motion sensors at my office went off so they sent me an alert. Somebody must've let a gnat in because it's buzzing around near the cameras, setting my alerts off," he flashed the phone in front of my face.

"Oh your office space is so nice and flowy. You decorated that yourself though, didn't you?" I cringed a little as I spoke and felt bad for showing my dissatisfaction.

"Yeah man, you trying to say my shit trash?" Xan chuckled.

"I mean... if I'm being honest, you can run me by Target right now and I could grab a few things and make it look one thousand times better than it does right now," I bragged.

"Shit come on then. I thought I did a good job but if you say it's ugly, I'll pay you to go to Target and grab some stuff so you can fix it tonight. My shit can't be fucked up while I'm dating an interior decorator," Xan stood from his stool at the bar and placed two hundred dollar bills on the bar.

"Wait, right now?"

"That's what you said, so let's go," he challenged.

I grinned and hopped off of my stool and allowed Xan to lead me out of the bar. Once we were seated in his Benz, I looked over at him. He was so handsome, laidback, and carefree. I loved every bit of it too. When we pulled up at Target, we immediately realized the store was closed, it was a little after eleven o'clock and we missed them.

"I guess I'll have to book you in the proper manner so you can get my office into tip top shape," Xan stated.

"I guess you will," I chuckled as he headed back in the direction of my house.

When we made it home, I turned on the tv but I wasn't paying it any attention. I was already online looking at various items for Xan's office. His nosey ass looked down at my phone and removed it from my grasp. "Nah, we aren't working. How do you go out to unwind, drink all of them damn lemon drops, and then come home and try to do shit for work?"

"I was just trying to make sure that I had a few ideas to show you once we sobered up," I clarified with a nervous smile.

The stare that Xan gave me forced my breathing to hitch. This man's handsome face, perfectly groomed beard, and laid back demeanor caused my yoni to leak profusely. We kissed on many different occasions but this time was different as Xan leaned in and initiated an earth shattering kiss. Our tongues ignited a deep passion between us. I experienced a foreign surge of emotions that made me feel all fuzzy on the inside. Every nerve in my body was alive and our surroundings faded in the distance, leaving me to focus on the rhythm of our breathing and the synchronized motions between our tongues. With my lips conjoined to Xan's, I repositioned myself so I was straddling him with my arms flung across his shoulders and around his neck. Just like our first date on the yacht, I was craving more than this kiss and was prepared to go all the way.

"I thought you would be over here distraught, waiting for me to make it home safely, but you over here trying to get that lil pussy beat," Yola's voice sounded off behind me.

We were clearly too engrossed in the kiss, ignoring our surroundings that we didn't hear the door open. When I turned around to lay eyes on Yola, the kiss left me feeling dizzy and unable to think straight for a moment. Clearing my throat, I attempted to gather my emotions and clear my jumbled thoughts. I wasn't moving fast enough because before I knew it, Mrs. Latifah and Mr. Al were in the doorway as well. The sight of my second set of parents gave me the nudge I needed to pull myself together and remove myself from Xan's lap. I quickly pulled a pillow over Xan's lap because I felt his hard dick beneath me and we were embarrassed enough.

"Yola!" I whimpered, rushing over to embrace my big mouth sister in the tightest hug. Tears filled both of our eyes, the ying to my yang was back and I looked over Yola's shoulder at Dro and mouthed, "thank you."

"You want us to leave and give y'all the house to yourselves? I didn't forget that freaky shit that you were talking about while you were drunk leaving King's."

My body tensed up because I was embarrassed about my actions last night but then I immediately relaxed because my sister was back, physically and mentally. That crazy bitch Priscilla didn't break her spirit or attitude.

CHAPTER 7

Dro

"I know you said you want me to relax but I'm fine. I want to open up my shop today," Yola whined, stomping in the middle of her lil ass bedroom.

"You think you about to go run the streets because I said I was going to be gone for a few hours?" I laughed at her audacity.

"Opening up my shop is not running the streets," Yola rolled her pretty ass eyes.

"Ion give a fuck about that bullshit you talking about or them lil ass feet stomping. You sitting the fuck down for a minute, the fuck I look like letting you out of my sight after what just happened? Them ugly ass hoes can wait on the wigs and lashes and all that other shit. You ain't been back for a full forty-eight hours, hang that shit up. You keep saying that you're fine but I want to make sure," I commented.

"Boy, my clients ain't ugly!" Yola chuckled.

"Well then they will be alright without all that extra shit. Real shit, most niggas don't even like all that extra shit y'all be doing."

"We don't do it for you dusty niggas, we do it for other bad bitches. Have you ever seen two bad bitches greet each other and twirl each other around bestowing compliments unto each other? That's what we do it for. Oh and the pictures, we definitely gotta flick up. Of course you dirty dick, trap all day, don't even change drawls ass niggas don't care for the shit. Y'all don't even care to pamper yourselves."

I removed my lips from her neck and glared at our reflection in the mirror. "You know I ain't no dirty nigga so don't lump me in with that bullshit. Sit yo sexy ass down and relax. Once the security is updated at the shop, y'all can open up. Oh, and Beast is going to retire from being my driver to working security at your shop. He is not to leave until the salon closes." I paused for a moment and rubbed my red chin hairs.

"Actually, saying that out loud, I thought of an even better idea. Beast can just be your driver from now on."

"No, see that sounds like a babysitter to me and that just don't sit right in my spirit. You just want him to spy on me, don't you?"

"Why I need him to spy on you Yola? You need to tell me something? If yo sneaky ass gone have other niggas sliding through the shop or meeting you at lunch, let me know right now and I can handle them while I'm out today so you don't have to worry about succumbing to temptation," I expressed, pushing her closer to the dresser while pressing my dick against her ass.

"No, get off of me. You wanna start talking shit so you can fuck me all rough and shit. No, I'm not with it, I have an attitude now," Yola spun around, folding her arms across her chest. "Dro! You are cutting into my money."

"Aye, stop talking to me like I'm a broke ass nigga. I paid the ladies what they would've made this week plus all of the money they had to return in the deposit fees. Them hoes probably had them same bitches pull up to get their hair, lashes, and shit done at the crib like they were doing while the shop was closed. As for you, you swipe my motha fuckin' cards more than me so I definitely don't wanna hear that shit. You are on rest and relaxation orders until at least Friday."

"Ughhhhhh! It's so hard dealing with yo simple ass."

"Well you know what they say, anything worth having ain't easy," I grinned, gripping my dick. "Now come on and sit on the dresser, you see how hard my shit is."

Yola pulled her pants down with an attitude and I definitely fucked that mean mug off of her face. An hour later, I left Beast at the crib with Yola and Anya while I headed across town to one of Vinny's spots. With all of the twists and turns I faced yesterday while dealing with my mom and Yola, I completely forgot that Vinny had Ross tied up somewhere waiting to be put out of his misery.

Although he wasn't the caliber of man that would ever pose a threat to me, I couldn't let him walk away after that shit he pulled outside of the restaurant. Plus my niggas already snatched him up off the streets so there was no coming back from that now. On the ride over, I put another blunt in the air as an incoming call from my contractor came through.

"Y'all better not be calling my phone with no bullshit," I answered, ready to make a detour to fuck somebody up.

"No sir, Mr. King, everything is done. I'm not sure if you read the last line of the email. We were supposed to conduct the walk through at noon but it's almost one o'clock and I have to get to another meeting."

"Shit, I forgot all about that. I ain't gone make it over there but check it, if my shit ain't immaculate after all of the random delays, got me sleeping in hotels and shit, I'mma come burn yo crib down with you inside."

"I... uummm... I promise the renovations will be up to your standard," he assured me.

"Say less," I ended the call because Pinky was calling on my other line.

"Wassup, Pinky?"

"Hey, Dro, I just wanted to let you know that your mother is checked into the rehab and I got her everything that they said she would need. I'm texting you the number of the facility so you will know it's your mom when she calls."

"Nah, Ion wanna talk to her, keep that mufuckin' number to yourself."

"Ummm... okay, I understand. How is Yola?"

"She's doing good. Trying to leave the house and shit to open that shop like she didn't just go through some traumatic shit. I ain't having that though. Can you do me one more favor?"

"You know I got you."

"Can you book us a massage at my house with that masseuse bitch Xan uses? Tell her I want the entire setup like she did for Anya. Champagne, chocolate covered strawberries, and all that shit. Plus I need you to grab a steak and lobster dinner from somewhere and setup a candlelight dinner in my dining room."

"Yay! That must mean your house is finally finished. What time do you want me to set this up for?" Pinky queried.

"Yeah, the contractors just told me my shit was done and Yola ain't never been to my crib before so I want to make it special. I need at least four hours. So let's say six o'clock. Tell the masseuse if she can bring a friend, we can do a couples massage type of thing."

"Let's do seven just in case I get stuck in traffic or something," she suggested.

"That'll work. I'll talk to you later."

We disconnected the call and I finished my blunt in solitude for the remainder of the drive. When I pulled up to Vinny's spot on the deserted streets in the middle of nowhere, I gripped my gun and headed inside.

"Wassup bih," Vinny dapped me up before leading me into the backroom where Ross was tied up.

Flicking on the lights, Ross' eyes grew wide when they connected with mine. I was a big nigga, but Ross was a fucking giant. At six-six, his tall ass was tied to a metal chair looking uncomfortable as fuck. My knees started creaking at the sight of him in the awkward position. He mumbled something with the silver strip of duct tape covering his mouth.

"I only came here to look you in your eyes before you took your last breath. The last time we saw each other, you were throwing out threats like you forgot who the fuck I was." Vinny handed me a gun and Ross squirmed around in the chair for less than five seconds before I put a bullet through his skull. Vinny took the gun and wiped it down before we exited the room.

"You really been coming the fuck through for a nigga," I commented after Vinny called the clean-up crew.

"Anybody got word about that nigga Zack?" I questioned.

"Nah, they looking for his people but it looks like they been moved away, so I expanded the search with some of our connections outside of Central Florida."

When we passed all of the phones we confiscated at Priscilla's cabin off to Xan's private investigator, it didn't take long for us to connect the dots. Edward was the younger brother to Zack and when we showed Yola the picture, she immediately confirmed that he was the one who took off on the dirt bike.

Zack used to work for me when I was gaining motion in these

streets. Afterwhile, I started hearing that Zack was playing with his nose so I had to let him go. That shit was so long ago and we were never that close. I was probably around Zack a few times when we had an organization wide meeting which was extremely rare because I never wanted my entire team in one spot at the same time. The big mystery was how in the fuck Zack got mixed up in this bullshit with my mama but I was going to find out right before I ended his life.

"How is everything with your girl and the baby?" I pried, getting my mind off the murderous thoughts swirling around in my head.

"They cool, she's at home on bed rest. My mama and her mama at the crib going back and forth all damn day. I gotta put one of them out tonight and that's going to cause a whole other problem," he rubbed his temples and I laughed at his ass because his mama and mother in-law were always into it about some petty shit. "How is your girl?"

"She straight, trying to run the streets like ain't shit happen."

"One thing about these women, they gone try it," Vinny added.

"Most definitely. So wassup man? You think you're ready for the big leagues?"

"Been ready and I'm going to stay ready."

"That shit might be falling in your lap sooner than you expected. This position is going to come with a lot of responsibilities and a shit load of headaches but if you want it, it's yours. I meet with my uncle on the third of the month and you gone slide through Mexico with me so I can make the introductions and then it's on. That shit with Yola opened my eyes and there is no time like now for me to step to the side. I got a shorty that Ion never wanna bring danger near. If you don't listen to shit else I say, remember this. Get your money and stay the fuck outta the way."

"Already," Vinny nodded his head and dapped me up before I exited the spot.

The next stop was to check the progress on my crib. It was Wednesday and they promised my shit was going to be ready today. If my crib wasn't done, I was going in somebody's jaw and Xan would just have to deal with the consequences later. I took the hour drive to my home with all the random ass middle of the day traffic and pulled up to see that they seemed to be true to their word.

Using my key to unlock the door, I sauntered through the foyer then my state of the art gym and finally entered the indoor basketball court. This shit was perfect. When I was a young jit, basketball was the dream I held onto to keep me sane. After Big Xan went to prison and I was left alone with Priscilla, I always said if I could make it to the league, I'd have my own money. My skills were superb for a youngin' but I sustained a few injuries in high school and that shit became a thing of the past.

I still played basketball for recreational purposes but the opportunities to do that became far and few once I claimed my seat at the head of Florida's drug game. When I started making real money, my goal was to own a home with an indoor basketball court, the mission was now complete and I was ready to enjoy the fruits of my labor. Pulling out my phone I shot Yola a text.

Me: I got some shit planned for us. Get dressed in something you can take off quick and be ready by six.

Good Pussy Yola: You know the way to my heart don't you?

Me: Duh, that's why I'm yo nigga.

I slid my phone back into my pocket and toured the remainder of the house to ensure that everything was in place and those motha fuckas didn't steal shit. After doing a quick walk through, I showered and changed into something comfortable before going to pick up Yola. I couldn't wait for her to see this shit.

A little after seven, I had Yola in the passenger seat with a sleep mask over her eyes as we approached my compound. Yola was complaining about her lashes at first but she quickly realized that I wasn't trying to hear that shit so she shut her mouth. I killed the engine and assisted Yola out of the car. Once we were positioned with the perfect view of my house, I pulled the mask off and braced for her reaction to the massive home.

"And if you fucked up my lashes I'mma fuck you up," Yola talked shit, batting her left eye before taking in her surroundings.

"I didn't fuck your lashes up and even if I did, you can't beat my ass, Yola," I slapped her ass with so much force that her body jumped and she emitted that sweet moan like she did every time.

"Whose house is this?" Yola scanned the home, landscape, and the cars in the driveway.

The Range Rover, Rolls Royce, and Lamborghini were just the tip of the iceberg. I was a car connoisseur and owned eight additional cars. A few old schools, classic cars, and muscle cars completed the collection.

"Ours," I avowed. "I told you when you saw my shit, you was gone come by to visit then try to move in my shit. Now that shit ain't a thought, it's a demand... welcome home, Yola. My girl can't be staying in that lil house another nigga bought her," I leaned down and planted a kiss on her lips.

Yola could barely pick her fat ass mouth up off the ground. I was able to allow my feelings for Yola to flourish because I knew she had her own money and wasn't aware of the type of nigga she was really dealing with. Gripping her hand, Yola's feet trailed me into the house and through the foyer.

"Welcome to an evening of rest and relaxation," Pinky greeted us with a pair of white robes.

"Pick a room, get changed, and the masseuses are set up in the den. I'm going to grab dinner and I'll be back."

"Oh my God, Dro! I didn't think you had this type of thing in you," Yola squealed, planting a kiss on my cheek before accepting the robe from Pinky.

"I got anything in me for you girl," I assured her.

We changed into the robes and I led her into the den as she admired the portions of the home that she was able to catch a glimpse of.

"Good evening, I was informed that you are my regular Alexander King's brother. My name is Julia and this is my associate Leah, claim your tables, and we can get started," she greeted us.

I allowed Yola to pick which table and masseuse she wanted and I took what was left for me. The entire time we indulged in the relaxing experience, I held Yola's hand and locked eyes with her. This woman was perfect for me, she matched my energy mentally, physically, and sexually. Most other bitches probably would've ran far as fuck away from me after being kidnapped by Priscilla, and rightfully so. However, Yola was standing by me and everything that came with me.

After the massages, we sipped champagne and I fed her fine ass strawberries while Pinky got the dining room table setup for our evening. Another thing I loved about Yola was how secure she was in her position. Even the bitches I was just fucking on hated on Pinky, but not Yola. I explained to her early on that Pinky used to live next door to Xan when we were teens and we always looked out for her. She was like our sister and that was that. When she went to college and got her degree as an accountant, I paid for her services just like I did Dro. I knew my money was invested well because Pinky was behind my moves. The club thing wasn't my first idea for a business investment, but Pinky had a solid plan and it was something she was down to put the leg work into so I said fuck it, threw the money into the venture, and now that shit was running smoothly with Pinky behind the wheel. Being an accountant wasn't her first dream, owning a club was. Her father owned a club when she was younger and she was attempting to carry on the legacy.

After our pedicures, we went into the dining room and thanked Pinky for the beautiful setup. Yola's favorite color was gold so the room was decked out in that shiny shit. Watching Yola smile from ear to ear showing off all of her perfect teeth in her mouth underneath the light from the chandelier made me feel slightly better because I felt like I had to put in a lot of work to make up for Priscilla's bullshit. This was just the start though, we had a lifetime to go.

"I really appreciate you for taking the time to plan out this relaxing evening," Yola leaned over to plant a kiss on my lips after we finished eating the lobster, steak, and mashed potatoes. "I've been so busy with getting Yo's Beauty Lounge together that I haven't had time to pamper myself like I usually do. This was much needed."

"Yeah and everything else," I reached across the table and gripped her hand.

"How are you feeling for real?" I questioned.

"I'm okay, I really wish that people would stop asking. I just want to get back to my normal life. If you really want to make me feel better then you would let me open my shop tomorrow."

"Not gone happen. You keep saying you straight but that was some traumatic shit."

"It was, but I made it out. Have you guys heard anything about Zack?" Yola queried.

"He never went back to the cabin and the only living family he had was his brother. Until that snake ass nigga is in the dirt, I'm keeping you close. On my soul, nobody will ever be in the position to cause you harm again."

Yola silently nodded her head and I leaned over to retrieve a gold gift bag that sat on the empty chair next to me. Placing it on the table in front of her, I watched as Yola pulled the black box out of the bag. Her eyes swiveled from me then back down to the gift box before she flipped it open, exposing the diamond tennis necklace and bracelet.

"I love it!" Yola squealed, pulling the jewelry from the box. I helped her secure the jewelry in place and she stood from the table, scanning the room. "Where is the closest mirror so I can see what it looks like on me?"

"Come on, let me give you a quick tour," I pulled her away from the dining room and we went into the sitting room, then the theater room, and the gym that took so much time to build. Ascending the double staircase, we went into the second level of the home but I took her fine ass straight to the master bedroom and in the bathroom. Pointing at the ceiling, I watched Yola's eyes connect with her reflection in the mirror. She gawked at a lot of the features in the home but I knew she'd love that one the most.

"Oh yeah, I'm going to have hella photo shoots all up and through yo crib."

"As long as you let me fuck you all up and through the crib," I commented.

"We should get started now," Yola suggested, pulling me back into the bedroom.

Licking my lips, I lifted her thick ass off of the ground and she wrapped her legs around my waist while she fed me her tongue. Easing down on top of Yola, she pulled her robe open and I gently massaged her titties while easing my dick inside of her. I swear this pussy got better every time I found myself in it. With each thrust, I was attempting to pour my heart and soul into Yola and I prayed she felt that shit too. Her hips bucked beneath me and I felt her break the kiss. Her hands roughly rubbed up and down my back as her lustful moans filled the silent home. Going deeper, I peered into Yola's eyes as my phone rang. Ignoring that shit, I wrapped my arms around Yola so she could get on top.

Slapping her ass, Yola took over, riding my dick until we both nutted. Drained and out of breath, my phone rang again but I ignored it and rubbed my hand up and down Yola's back but she wasn't having that.

"So who the fuck keeps calling you this late at night?" Yola sat up on the bed to nudge my head.

"Ion know, let me see," I extended my arm over the edge of the bed and retrieved my phone from the nightstand. It was Vinny calling me back to back. Irritation immediately spread within me because I knew there were only two possible reasons for Vinny to blow my shit up. Either something was out of order and I would have to get up or somebody fucked some shit up and was in prison. No matter which option it was, I knew I wouldn't be able to lay up with Yola and christen the crib like I planned to.

"Nigga, this shit better be important." I answered the phone as Vinny called again.

"It is, we just grabbed that nigga. He was in the city searching for your mama. He actually had the nuts to pull up to one of the spots with his chest poked out looking for you. Demanding answers about Priscilla and shit."

"Sayless. Give me an hour," I disconnected the call.

As soon as I did that shit Yola started her bullshit. "See this where you got me fucked up at!" Yola hopped from the bed and screamed, them big juicy titties all up in my face. "Give me the keys to one of those cars out there. I don't give a fuck which one, just hand over some fucking keys, nigga, because I'm going home. This was supposed to be our first night together in your nice ass house..."

"Our nice ass house," I interrupted and that further pissed Yola off because she groaned and threw her robe over her shoulders and tied it in the front, fucking up my view. "What? This *our* shit. I'm going to have you added to the deed. If anything happens to me, I wanna make sure my shit is split between you and Xan. I'm serious, bae."

LAKIA

"Yo pea brain ass know that's not what I'm talking about!"

"Bae, chill. I got a few loose ends to tie up then you're mine for good. That nigga Zack who was with my mom is in the city so you know I gotta handle that, whether you have an attitude or not."

At the mention of Zack, it was like a switch was flipped and her attitude dissipated. Yola went into the bathroom and I heard the shower water turn on. "You want me to tell Xan to bring Anya over here to keep you company?" I inquired, stepping into the bathroom. Yola already made herself at home in my jacuzzi tub and fuck if I ain't wanna get in there with her.

"Yes, I would appreciate that very much," Yola bubbled.

"I got you. You're safer here than anywhere else in the city so I don't mind leaving you here alone. Motion sensors start at the driveway. Only Xan, Pinky and Beast know where this spot is and I have cameras everywhere. Bulletproof windows, Forretress series forced entry prevention doors at all entrances and exits. That's another reason why I want you here."

I leaned down and initiated a deep kiss that almost made me want to slide into the tub with her. Forcing myself to be responsible, I was dressed and on my way out of the door shortly afterwards. Speeding through traffic, I couldn't believe Zack came to us. A large part of why I was keeping Yola so close was the fact that I hadn't been able to touch Zack.

Crossing the threshold to Vinny's spot in the middle of nowhere, that feeling of déjà vu slapped me in the face. Just earlier today, it was Ross and now it was Zack. "Where he at? I'm trying to handle this shit quick and get home to my girl."

"In the back where they always are," Vinny informed me with a head nod. "I did have to knock his ass out because you know he's a big nigga."

"Did he say anything to them niggas on the block?"

"Nah, they just said he was looking for you or Priscilla and them young boys drug his ass into one of them trap houses and beat his ass until we got there," Vinny detailed, flipping a switch to illuminate the dusty ass small bedroom. Plastic covered the room and I took a deep breath before kicking this nigga in his stomach.

Zack's body jerked and he emitted a few deep coughs while squirming around on the floor with his hands cuffed behind his back. "Where the fuck is Priscilla? What did you do to her?"

The way Priscilla's name rolled off of Zack's tongue triggered memories from the night I was knocking on death's door. He drug out that -la at the end of her name in such a hard dramatic manner that there was no way I was mistaking that shit. My breathing became erratic, my fists clenched so tight that I felt like my body was bound to explode into millions of microscopic pieces. I lunged forward, fists swinging chaotically as I tried to knock this nigga's head off his shoulders. All of these years later, I would never forget the way that her name rolled off of this nigga's tongue as I fought for my life in the middle of my bedroom floor. Zack was unrecognizable from the amount of force that I applied to his face with each punch.

Easing up off of Zack, I stepped back because his blood was getting all over me and I didn't want to make shit worse. I never got this emotional but realizing that *this* was the nigga who almost took my life hit different. Zack spat blood onto the floor as he looked up at me with his eyes narrowed in anger. His hands were still cuffed behind his back but I didn't give a fuck, there was no sympathy or sense of fairness after the way he violated me on two separate occasions. The fact that Priscilla was still hanging around the same nigga that almost took my life didn't surprise me but that bitch stung my soul every chance she got. I didn't know how much longer this bitch could continue walking around, causing destruction, and getting away with it because she was the offspring of a cartel boss.

Zack couldn't speak, he was too weak, but he definitely murdered me a few times with his eyes. Pulling my gun out, I stepped over his body and he weakly turned over, I guess he didn't want to see the bullet coming. When I caught a glimpse of Zack's hands tied behind his back I was served another blow to the heart. Forced onto his fat ass finger was an extremely distinctive ring. I would recognize that shit anywhere because I had one to match it back at the crib.

The gold ring was shaped into the head of a jaguar and there was a red ruby clamped between the jaguar's sharp teeth. My matching ring at home was identical but there was a black onyx clamped between the jaguar's teeth. Dropping my gun on the side of me, I used my strength to pull the ring off of his sausage fingers while breathing like a fucking maniac.

"You good Dro?" Vinny quizzed and I ignored his ass.

Ripping the ring off of Zack's finger, I gripped my gun and stood upright. Glancing at the ring's inscription engraving, I felt sick to my stomach reading the words that mi Papá always recited to us. *We are predators, strong, and ferocious.* When I turned eighteen and entered the dope game, my older cousin Maceo, my Uncle Macario's son, came to Florida as a form of oversight but he loved it here so he decided to stay and we were running shit. After our first year in business, mi Papá gifted us these rings because jaguars were his thing, he saw them as a sign of strength. Here this nigga was in possession of my deceased cousin's ring.

"Aye!" I knelt down again and gripped Zack's shirt and roughly slapped his face, praying that he would come out of whatever daze he was in. "Did you kill Maceo? Did Priscilla have anything to do with that shit? How did you get this ring?" I quizzed rapidly, shaking this nigga so he could give me an answer.

This nigga grinned at me and the sight of his bloody teeth told me everything I needed to know. Zack took a moment to muster up the strength to speak and the words that he chose to spit were the hard truth I'd been struggling to deal with.

"Priscilla setup every lick I hit. I came before you and your cousin Maceo. *I'm* her fucking family," he confirmed and I shoved his bitch ass to the ground.

Letting off two shots to his skull, I tossed the gun to the ground and looked at Vinny with murder in my eyes. He stepped to the side and allowed me out of the room without a word. My world was flipped upside down so many times in the last few days that I felt like my head was going to explode with all of these revelations.

I called Pinky on my way out of the spot and waited for her to answer. It was a little late but I needed to know where Priscilla was now. This piece of information was exactly what I needed to justify me putting her in the dirt. She chose drugs and a nigga over her family for the last time.

CHAPTER 8

Priscilla

This was my second day in rehab, a little under the forty-eight hour mark and just like the doctors informed me during the intake process, the withdrawal symptoms were at their peak. I can't tell you how many times I vomited or shitted my life away. The sweats and shakes weren't no joke either. Heroin recently became my vice because it was so damn cheap and we were broke as hell.

Thoughts of Zack flooded my mind and I prayed that he got away safely because that man owned my heart. I didn't know what I would do without him. Don't get me wrong, Big Xan was the love of my life, but he wasn't accessible to me and I'm not the *hold my man down, lonely* type. In five years when Big Xan would be released from prison, I'd happily leave Zack in the dust and get my shit together for my husband. For now, it was me and Zack against the world.

Zack was ten years my junior and I actually met him because of Dro. If Dro knew that we were creeping around he would've definitely lost his damn mind. When Dro first stepped into the game I got clean and stopped using coke at his request. However, it's difficult to kick a habit like coke and one night, I happened to run into Zack at a party. He worked for my son at the time and saw me in passing a few times because I was all up in Dro's business back then, making sure that shit was running correctly. So when Zack and I saw each other at the party, we offered one another cordial greetings.

I was planning to keep shit pushing but I quickly noticed that Zack was supplying party drugs. It was like I could taste the drugs as I spotted him conducting an exchange with another man in attendance. After a short internal debate, I decided to request a vial and the rest was history. Since I clearly was requesting the drugs for my personal pleasure, Zack felt comfortable letting me know that he dabbled in party drugs here and there at parties just to elevate his mood. Shortly afterwards, Dro gave Zack his walking papers because he had a zero tolerance for drug use amongst his team.

My mind drifted off to Dro and I thought back to the day that really changed my life and relationship with my son for good.

*"Dro, I'm your mother, how in the fuck do you think you get to tell me that I have to go to rehab in order for you to give me any money? If it wasn't for me then you wouldn't be in the position you are in! You **owe** me! **I** put you on! **I** trained you up!"*

"Ma, you got Uncle Macario to front me my first few bricks but I took off. I built this shit, I hustled my motha fuckin' ass off while you sat on your ass. I stand on that shit I said a year ago, if you're out of money, you better go check yourself into rehab. Until then, that shit dead with me. Only a real addict would sell their house and go on a coke induced trip that included a shopping spree and partying. You outta pocket and you're cut off until you get some help."

"Pendejo arrogante! (Arrogant idiot!)" I screeched into the phone and tossed it across the room with so much force that there was now a hole in the hotel room wall. The anger took over me and I didn't even realize that Zack was standing across from me. He ducked and the phone only missed his head by a few millimeters. Zack stood across the room, listening to my side of the conversation with my son while he smoked a cigarette with his shirt off.

"Mi amor, relax," he smirked, walking over to brush a few strands of my disheveled hair behind my ear.

"How am I going to relax Zack? We are out of money and I can't keep living like this," I whined, waving my arm around the two star hotel room. *"I'm used to living a certain lifestyle and this ain't it!"*

An entire year lapsed since Dro cut me off financially. At first I didn't give a fuck, it wasn't a big deal because I had plenty of tricks on my roster. Unfortunately, my coke usage was more prevalent and harder to hide so the affluent men that I used to bag weren't as generous. Hell, some of them wouldn't deal with me at all because of my drug usage. The handful that I still had were heavy coke abusers too so I usually just copped blow from them. Not only was I using the money and drugs that I squeezed out of these men for myself, I was also taking care of Zack and supplying the drugs to feed his addiction.

I fidgeted with my fingers for a few moments until that no longer satisfied my level of agitation. Hopping to my feet, I ran my hands through my red curls then massaged my temple. I was overwhelmed and my emotions were difficult to control. At that point, I was downright impulsive so the next words that fell out of my mouth were due to my lack of drugs and foresight.

"I bet his stupid ass didn't even change his locks, safe locations, or none of that shit. If he keeps fucking around I might have to rob him, show him that I brought him into this game and I could make it hard for him to thrive in it too. I taught him **everything**, I know **everything** about his operation. I could make shit real hard for him to move!"

After the words slipped from my lips, I saw Zack's eyes light up. "Let's do it then, bae," Zack coaxed at me, walking over in my direction. "If you know the code to the safe, we can be in and out quick as fuck while he is hanging out. Nobody gotta get hurt," he coerced me with that perfect smile.

We were two years into our situationship by then, down on our luck, and I loved this man so I was willing to betray my son to feed our drug habit. "Okay, but we have to do it tonight. He goes to Mexico to meet my brother on the third of every month so I know his house is empty now."

"Let's slide then," Zack gripped his gun and our ski masks from the dresser.

Yes, there were already two ski masks in the room because we'd robbed a few old ladies over the last few weeks to help us get by. When I say we were down bad, I meant that shit. With our essentials in hand, Zack drove the three hour drive from the cabin in Morriston to Dro's house in Tampa. It was a little after two o'clock in the morning when we pulled up and the streets were dark. The lights were off in Dro's house as expected.

"Alright, we gotta be in and out, these neighbors might call the cops if they see us getting out of the car in these ski masks."

"I love you, girl," Zack cooed, leaning over the seat to tongue me down. I had to pull back because he already had my pussy tingling and I'd be ready to sit on his dick before I knew it.

"I love you too. In and out," I repeated before hopping out of the car.

In hindsight, I don't know why the fuck I wore a ski mask. We approached the door and I used my spare key to enter the home. Once they looked at the security footage, Dro would've known that it was me because I was the only other person with a key to his house. Ascending the stairs at a rapid pace, we were making hella noise. It sounded like a damn stampede of niggas was ascending the stairs instead of just me and Zack. Unbeknownst to us, Dro was home and asleep in bed so the noise we were making tore him from his slumber. When we entered the bedroom, Dro let off wild shots until he emptied the clip and Zack returned fire. Dro's body slipped to the floor and blood instantly soaked the sheets beneath him.

"Fuck! Priscilla, open the safe so we can get the money and go!" Zack ordered.

Ignoring Zack's command, I rushed over to the bed and pulled the ski mask off of my face. The pained expression on Dro's face flipped to one filled with rage and indignation once he saw my face. Consumed with guilt, I wanted to sink into the hardwood floors and disappear but I couldn't. Dro was losing blood fast and I had to help my baby. The agitation from being sober and the craving for drugs disappeared for the first time in a long time. My mind was preoccupied with thoughts of saving my son's life.

"It's okay, Dro. Mommy is here, hold on for me, baby," I pleaded, applying pressure to the bullet holes in his chest with one hand while looking for my phone to call the police with my other hand. "I'm so sorry, I never would've done this if I thought that you were home."

"Priscilla! What's the combination to the safe?" Zack's voice interrupted the feelings I was expressing to Dro.

"Just call the police! I need to get him to the hospital!" I sobbed because I couldn't find my phone.

"Priscilla, we can't be here when the police pull up or we are going to jail. Give me the combination to the safe Priscilla and I'll grab some money and go call the cops but my phone is in the car."

"Ummmmm, try 01-13-90-55."

"Priscilla, that shit didn't work!" Zack based a few moments later.

"Try 89-43-23-76."

"That shit didn't work either! Let's go Priscilla, I hear sirens."

"Just take my ski mask and go! I need to make sure he gets to the hospital and is okay. I can't leave him like this."

"Fuck, alright. As soon as you can slip away from the hospital, do that. The nigga might be sick of your shit and tell the cops you were in on it when he wakes up."

"Okay."

Later on I found out that Dro was only home that day because he caught the flu. If it wasn't for Dro's illness mixed with the nighttime cold and flu medication he was taking, I'm positive he would've killed me and Zack that night because that was probably the only time his bullets didn't hit their intended targets.

Thinking about that dreadful evening increased my craving for any drug exponentially and I couldn't take that shit anymore. When I was high, the heinous shit I did was hastily forced to the back of my mind where those thoughts needed to remain. I desperately wanted to do right, I wanted to get clean for my son but not today. The memories were too dark, the craving was too staggering, and the regret was overwhelming. Hopping out of the bed, I grabbed the bag that contained the various jogger sets that Dro sent to the facility for me and exited the room.

"Good evening Ms. King, did you need something?" Chelsea, the nice nurse, was puzzled once she saw me in the hallway.

I ignored her ass and headed straight for the door while she called out behind me and attempted to get me to stay. The only thing on my mind was getting high. Since I was voluntarily in the rehab I knew they couldn't make my ass stay so I was out of that bitch. Once I rounded the building, I was so glad I did because Dro swerved in front of the building and jumped out like a mad man. If I was still inside there was no question the anger exuding from Dro would've been taken out on me.

Fight or flight kicked in and my ass took off running. Without a destination in mind, I jogged until I ran across a CVS that was still open and went inside to make a phone call. Dialing Zack's phone number, I tapped my foot and fidgeted with my ear lobe while I waited for my knight in shining armor to greet me. I was desperate and the more the phone rang, the higher my anxiety rose thinking about Dro finding me. The line kept ringing until it went to voicemail and I nervously tapped my foot continuously because I needed to get away from here as soon as possible.

There was so much for Dro to be angry about and I wasn't sure if Dro would spare me for a third time. I'm positive he only allowed me to continue breathing after Zack shot him because the doctors told him that if it wasn't for me applying pressure to his wounds, he might have bled out that night. When Dro was discharged from the hospital, he held me captive for a while, trying to get me to tell him who ran up in his house with me that evening, but I wouldn't give Zack up. I thought that Dro would kill me, however, he allowed me to live but told me never to come back to Tampa again.

I followed Dro's request, left town, and reached out to Big Xan's best friend, Tremaine, who secured the small cabin in Morriston as a favor to my husband. Up until recently, I only called Dro once a year in an attempt to make amends but my youth and looks were no longer getting me what it used to and I needed financial help badly. The light and water bill were behind and we didn't know where our next meal would come from. Placing a second and third call to Zack's phone, my fidgeting only increased.

I looked up from the phone to see judgment all over the cashier's face. I didn't give a fuck though. These tremors weren't a joke and I felt like I was knocking on death's door and the only thing on my mind was getting drugs in my system to help me ease these withdrawal symptoms. Without thinking, I grabbed the woman's shirt and placed the phone to her head.

"Unless you want me to bash your skull in, empty the fucking register."

WAP! WAP! WAP!

"Bitch if you don't get your bony ass the fuck outta here!" She screeched after hitting me with a three piece combo. I fell into the candy display behind me and watched in horror as she rounded the register. Scrambling to my feet, I ran out of the CVS at sonic speed like only a junkie could.

Mulling over my situation, I thought about Frank Russo. Luckily, I wasn't too far from his home and Frank always said he owed me big time for making the connection between him and my brother Macario last year. Also, Big Xan was the one who put everything together, it was my physical presence that sealed the deal. I pulled my shit together enough to have Macario believe that I was clean and he paid me a bonus for bringing him another client. There was no time like now to cash in. Moving my feet as fast as they would go, I didn't stop my light jog until I made it to Frank's home.

I stuck out like a sore thumb in this area on foot, shaking and scratching. The guard at the entrance of his neighborhood phoned

Frank and provided him with my name. Not only did Frank tell him to let me through the gate, the security guard begrudgingly drove me to the back of the neighborhood where Frank's massive home was positioned on his golf cart. I cashed in on my favor and then some after a brief conversation with Frank. He gave me a little coke to satisfy my craving and within a few hours, I was in the back of a black Tahoe headed to my cabin in Morriston to secure my passport then we continued the drive to Mexico. With a little money in my pocket, I was ready to start fresh, free of the drama in Florida. Kidnapping Yola and running up in Dro's house were both Zack's ideas and maybe it was truly time for me to separate myself from him as well. Absence didn't make the heart grow fonder while Zack was missing in action, it actually helped me gain a little clarity once the withdrawal symptoms slowed down and the high took over.

Once I arrived in Mexico, I went to my usual dealer's house. He was an older gentleman by the name of Mateo. I met him through Big Xan, we used to stop by to see him whenever we vacationed in Mexico. When Big Xan went to prison, I knew I could count on Mateo to supply me with drugs when I came to town. There was no way that he would tell Big Xan because he was too busy trying to get into my panties. Tonight, I used that to my advantage because I was aimlessly maneuvering the city without a plan. The last few years of my life mirrored this behavior as well and I knew I needed to figure my shit out. I burned so many bridges that I didn't have anyone to rely on. My son hated me, my brother and father stopped dealing with my bullshit a year after Big Xan went to prison, and Zack was a terrible influence on my life. I didn't have anyone to lean on but tonight, I would get high and sleep on Mateo's couch.

I took a shower and changed into another jogger set then relaxed my mind with a bump of coke. After traveling for over twenty-four hours, I just wanted to unwind. Exiting the bathroom, I claimed a seat on the couch across from Mateo and had to pause for a moment to refocus my eyes. My vision went blurry and Mateo's head broke into four identical pieces. Laying my head back on the couch, I tried to focus but couldn't for shit. My body seemed to go limp and then Mateo stood over me. The first thing that crossed my mind was this nasty nigga drugged me so he could rape me. However, Big Xan's voice sounded off and I immediately knew that my fate was even grimmer than I thought.

"You disappointed me Priscilla," Big Xan scoffed. "You are one *special* bitch, you know that right? You spent our son's college fund before he hit puberty, forced him into the drug game, and really did all that shit Xan said you did when he was a child. I was blinded by love but bitch, I can see clearly now. If I was out of prison, I would've killed you with my bare fucking hands, watched the life drain from your beautiful face as I crushed your windpipes. I sat down and did this time and you were supposed to lead the family, but you didn't do shit but turn into a catalyst for destruction in our son's life. You were never the bitch I thought you were and I'm not about to let you get away with the shit you put Xan and Dro through. I guess I'll see you in hell bitch."

Big Xan spoke some extremely harsh words but I was woman enough to accept them. Although I wasn't ready, I had no choice but to accept my fate as my body convulsed uncontrollably and the darkness consumed me. At least my trail of darkness and destruction was over.

CHAPTER 9

Anya

"Alright, are you ready to see your new office space?" I questioned Xan.

He was seated in his conference room since I was all up in his space holding true to my word to transform the place. Xan looked from the laptop to me and offered me a bright smile before standing to his feet.

"I'm definitely ready to see what type of magic you worked in there," he stood up and trailed me down the hallway.

Since Yola was back home safely and things seemed to be getting back to normal, I spent my time transforming Xan's entire office into a professional oasis. Throughout this week, I updated his entrance, hallway, and conference room. Now the final updates were in Xan's office and a twinge of nervousness crept up on me because this was the most significant room due to the fact that this was where he spent most of his time. I watched anxiously as Xan stepped inside of the office and allowed his eyes to observe every detail in the room.

"I hope that you like the new colors. I went with black because it exudes power and you are definitely a powerful attorney. Plus I combined the green to add a little balance in the room. It's a stable color related to growth, stability, and affluence." As I rambled on about the meaning behind his new color scheme Xan stared at me silently, making me wonder what the hell was going on inside of his head. Although we'd spent a lot of time together since his house caught on fire, this man still had a way of sending my nerves into a tizzy. Fidgeting with my fingers, I posed the dreaded question. "I know a lot of people don't care about that type of stuff so I'll stop rambling. Do you like it?" I faltered.

"I love it," Xan leaned down and graced my lips with the sweetest kiss. "Stop downplaying what you do and the effort you put into your shit. Talk about the colors and all that shit with your chest out. I noticed how much you second guess and doubt your talents and I don't know why because you're dope as fuck. You gotta start exuding confidence, especially when it comes to your work."

"Do I really do it that often?" I paused to wonder aloud.

"Hell yeah. I can tell you two instances off the top of my head when you did that shit. When I helped you put together that dining room, you were so nervous and second guessing yourself. The night we had our first date, I asked you how did things go at the shop and you said something like, 'Yola loved it and Dro paid you so you thought you did good.' I wanna hear that same energy you had when you were drinking lemon drops and confidently telling me my shit was trash and you could slide through Target and do a better job than I did. Talk yo shit at all times."

I chuckled slightly, allowing Xan's words to settle in. He was right, I put on a brave face sometimes, but I often lacked confidence. "Okay, you're right," I admitted, holding my head up high as we stepped into the office. "I incorporated elephants on your bookshelf as place holders because I know that they are special to you," I pointed out with the extension of my acrylic nails in that direction.

"Does your knowledge on color schemes influence what color you get your nails?" Xan questioned, looking at my nails.

Snickering, I examined my hot pink nails that were accentuated with crystals. "I think I allowed color psychology to influence me a little with my decision."

"What does the color pink mean?" Xan pried. The fact that he cared to learn was special to me because this was the type of geeky shit that I never shared with anyone because I didn't think people cared.

"Well pink pulls the passion and energy from the color red and combines it with the purity of the color white to create the playful, feminine, and romantic color."

"That's what's up, I love that color on you. So what are you planning to get into when you leave here today?"

"I planned to go to pick up Rex from home then drive over to Dro's house since Yola asked me to come over. What about you?"

"I have to meet with a new client today and then I'll be meeting with the realtor to see a few more houses." Xan detailed.

"So you're in a little rush to get from under my roof?"

"Nah, but Ion want your parents looking at me like a bum that's trying to live rent free under their daughter's crib you know. Plus I thought you were getting tired of me."

"Not at all. I've enjoyed you being there. Plus I know Yola is about to move in with Dro. I can feel it, they are already practically joined at the hip," I confessed.

"Yeah probably," Xan agreed as his office phone rang.

"Okay, I'm going to let you grab that and get out of your hair," I cooed, planting a kiss on his lips before exiting the office.

Waving to Preme on my way out of the office I couldn't stop mulling over the future. Life at home without Yola was boring as hell. Being entrepreneurs with the freedom of time was a freeing experience but I was terrified of that shit now. Xan was already looking at new places since there was no salvaging his house and if Yola left, my ass would be stuck in that house all by myself.

I drove home, picked up Rex, and let Yola know I was on my way over there. It was an hour drive from my own house and I allowed my Mary J Blige playlist to serenade me for the duration of the drive. When I arrived at the address my mouth almost hit the damn floor.

"Damnnnnnnn this house is massive," I swooned over Dro's home as I pulled into the circular driveway. My random outburst caused Rex to hop up and take a gander out of the window.

Parking behind an old school car, I pulled Rex into my arms before exiting the car. Yola's loud ass came rushing out with a huge smile on her face. "Sisterrrrrrr!" She screamed, rushing over in my direction.

I ran to meet her halfway and we shared a dramatic hug in the driveway. "I knew Dro had money but geesh, he has that real shmoney," I slapped Yola a high five.

"Yes, I did hit the jackpot with the lil leprechaun," Yola bragged.

"Come on, let me give you a tour of my humble abode," Yola grabbed my hand to lead me and Rex inside.

"Girl, ain't shit humble about this house. Of all the homes I've decorated, this is the biggest house I've ever been to. Give me the details," I urged, scanning the entryway.

"It's a five bedroom, seven and a half bathroom home with a four car garage, gym, and theater room. Girl, Dro has ten cars so he really should've invested in more garage space instead of an indoor basketball court."

"Damnnnnnn! Show me the indoor basketball court. I've never been inside of a house with an indoor basketball court before."

Yola gave a brief tour on the way to the basketball court and I couldn't even lie, Dro's home decor was impressive so I knew he didn't decorate it himself. Once we were inside Yola grabbed a basketball and I placed Rex on the ground so he could run free. We weren't even the basketball type but we dribbled the balls and shot the ball towards the hoop, missing every time.

"You're glowing," I pointed out, dribbling my basketball in front of me.

"Yeah. That's what love tends to do to you," Yola beamed.

"That means you're going to move in and leave me all alone?" I whined. "We just moved into this house together and now you're about to ditch me and move wayyyy out here."

"We are going to have to cut the cord at some point, Anya," she sighed, plopping down on the floor and I followed suit.

"Oh yeah and everything has been so crazy that I haven't had the chance to ask you why the fuck did Tazz tell me you decorated his house?"

"Ughhhhh," I rolled my eyes. "Tazz should've told you that he's a sneaky ass nigga. He booked under his real name so that was the only reason I went to his house. How was I supposed to know that his name was Jameis? I didn't know that Jerricka was his wife until the final day when he was there to pay me. The walls were bare since they wanted me to redo everything so there weren't any family photos hanging up or anything like that," I explained. "You know I would never do no weirdo shit like that and you were on to the next so I wasn't trying to trigger you. I know how you used to feel about him."

"Nigga's really ain't shit for real," she quipped. Rex limped over to us and Yola wrapped her arm around me. "Ion even want to think about it. Past situations give me flashbacks that I don't need since Dro and I are getting serious, he unofficially asked me to marry him after everything that happened with Priscilla."

"What did you say?" I burst with excitement for Yola, sitting up on my knees to offer her my full attention.

"I said yes but he has to really come with it for me to mean what I said for real. You know I need a big rock if he wants to sit me on the bench for the rest of my days," she spoke confidently. I always loved how confident she was and I needed some of that shit to rub off on me.

"I'm so happy for you. I never thought I would see the day when Yola settled down."

"Shit, me either, but I can see you and Xan doing the same in the near future. If it's not Xan then it will be someone else. Damn, we are about to enter the next stage of our lives and I didn't even think about that until just now."

"Yeah, you're right. I'm so happy for you and Dro," I simpered. "Change is hard but I'm getting with it. My ass is just going to be lonely once Xan finds a house. He was looking yesterday and is scheduled to see another house today."

"At the end of the day I'm still going to be your sister and bff all wrapped up in one. Nothing is going to change the bond we have, lil sis. I love you," Yola expressed, pulling me into her chest and planting a kiss on my forehead.

"I love you too."

"Plus I'm not moving in with Dro that fast. I already told him I'm coming home at least twice a week. I would miss you and Rex too much," Yola confessed, pulling Rex into her lap and he instantly went crazy rolling around, licking her, and wagging his tail rapidly. "On top of that, I think he just wants me to move in so he can keep me safe. His crazy ass mom left the rehab facility yesterday and he already has Beast driving me most places. I don't want this to turn into some pity shit, you know?"

"I don't think Dro would ever treat you any type of way out of pity. His rude ass mouth couldn't fake it if he wasn't experiencing these types of feelings for you for real."

LAKIA

"Well only time will tell. Besides, I'm not sure if I'm ready for a man to be all up in my space twenty-four seven just yet. I went from being in these skreets to a nigga trying to turn me into a kept bitch, Ion know about that. For now though, let's go in this big ass kitchen and make dinner together. Find out what time Xan will be done and we can do a couples dinner, the four of us for the first time."

"Okay, show me the kitchen, I know the shit is niceeeeee," I squealed.

CHAPTER 10

Yola
One Week Later

"Bae, do you know how much I love you?" I cooed, pulling a black crop top over my head and high waist jeans over my thick thighs.

"Better be with all your fuckin' heart," Dro eased up behind me and planted a kiss on my neck. Chills went straight down my spine and somehow wound up in my pussy cat. Dro's lips were definitely the match that lit my inner freaky flames.

"All that plus some," I assured him before melting into his chiseled chest. "Since I know how much you love me, I know that you will do almost anything for me. That includes walking Rex and accompanying him to his vet appointment. I promised Anya that I would take him to his appointment because she had a consultation scheduled this morning, but I just received a last minute priority booking and you know that comes with a nice lil added fee. Xan is in court today and you're the only unemployed adult in the group so it seems fair that you take him," I rubbed my hands together thinking about the money.

"Yo fat head ass trying to take advantage now," Dro released the grip he had on me and hit me with the side eye. "You want me to walk that slow cripple motha fucka down the block and take him to his weekly vet appointment. I didn't even wanna bring my ass to this house but you know I can't sleep in the bed without you."

"And you know I can't just abandon Anya and leave her here all of the time. I'm coming home at least twice a week so she isn't always alone," I reminded him.

Dro was trying to move me all the way into that big ass house so he could have me all to himself. I loved sharing my space with him around the clock but I wasn't prepared to cut the cord with Anya. We were joined at the hip until Dro came along. Not only was it hard for me to be without my sister for that long, I also worried about her living alone. Although Xan was living with her now, he was in the process of looking for a new home so that shit would be coming to an end soon.

"Anya ain't alone, she be with Xan all of the time. Shit she better fuck Xan so they can make their shit official and move in together because we can't keep doing this," Dro interrupted my thoughts, motioning around the room.

"Boy," I laughed but I could tell from his face that he didn't see shit funny and that only made me cackle harder. "I'm sure Anya doesn't have to fuck Xan for him to invite her to live with him. Just because you had to give up the dick to reel me in don't mean nothing."

"Nah, you mean you had to give me some of that pussy. I had you bussin' that shit open on my office desk before you even knew my name, don't get amnesia now."

"No, I had you putting in the work, flipping my thick ass around that office, you the one who seemed to forget. Even broke me off a lil something something afterwards, practically stalked me for the pussy and took me on a vacation within a week. I'm the motha fuckin' GOAT, baby, and don't you forget it," I stuck my tongue out after proving my point. "Now mind your business and let them move at their corny speed."

"Shit we grown, you either fuckin' or you ain't," Dro shrugged, opening the door to let Rex hobble into the room. "How long this lil nigga gone be fucked up in this cast and shit anyways?"

"I don't know but you can ask the vet when you get there. I'm headed to the shop with my babysitter Beast," I informed Dro with a peck on the lips. "Dinner is on me tonight, sugar daddy."

"I want lemon pepper wings from Peabody's and you gotta watch *Jackie Brown* with me when we get home."

I rolled my eyes because I was tired of Samuel L. Jackson. Every day Dro wanted to watch a different movie from Samuel L. Jackson's catalog and I was sick of seeing his cursing ass on a daily basis. Over the last week since I moved in with Dro, we'd watched *Pulp Fiction, Jackie Brown, Shaft, A Time To Kill,* and *The Negotiator* more times than I'd like to admit. Dro told me that Samuel L. Jackson was his favorite

CRUSHING ON THE PLUG NEXT DOOR 2: FINALE

actor since he was a kid, it was no wonder his mouth was so damn reckless. However, I didn't complain. I nodded my head, grabbed my purse, and headed to the living room because I needed Dro to do me this favor.

"I'm all dressed and ready to hit the town," I sang, exiting my bedroom.

Beast stood from the couch and led me outside to Dro's Rolls Royce. Easing into the backseat, I could get used to this shit. I'd grown accustomed to men sending nice cars to pick me up for dates here and there, but this had become an everyday thing and I cherished the daily experience now. While Beast drove, I posted content on social media, checked emails, answered DMs, and all of that good shit.

We arrived at the shop shortly afterwards and I still couldn't believe that this was now my reality. Yo's Beauty Lounge was in full swing after all of the bullshit I'd endured, I deserved the smooth transition after we pushed the opening date back. Disabling the alarm, Beast sat in his chair near the entrance and a few minutes later, the other stylists trickled in greeting me with their beautiful smiles. Since I was scheduled to perform a lace install I already had my supplies out and ready.

Right on time, the chimes above the door sounded off and I looked up to see Jerricka, Tazz's wife, enter the building with her natural hair up in a high bun and a wig in her hand. I tensed up for a moment because a part of me felt like she was there to confront me about Tazz but she smiled and greeted me with a firm handshake.

"Good morning, Yola. Thank you so much for squeezing me in at the last minute. I have an event to attend with my husband tonight, but Shay Styles is my usual stylist and she had to cancel at the last minute so she recommended you," Jerricka greeted me.

I relaxed slightly and smiled, accepting the lace front wig that she held in her hand. Shay Styles was another dope ass stylist that I knew, so it was definitely plausible that she sent Jerricka my way but I was still uneasy about the situation. I didn't want to be that shiesty bitch doing a woman's hair, knowing I used to fuck on her nigga. However, Jerricka was here and I made a mental note to change the manner in which I accepted priority bookings. Usually, I had to approve a client when they requested a regular appointment but the priority or short notice booking didn't require an approval because they come with an additional three hundred dollar fee on top of the actual services.

Placing Jerricka's wig on my station vanity, I led her over to the shampoo bowl and got started. She made small talk while I massaged her scalp and I just couldn't wait for this shit to be over. Halfway through her braid down other clients started to enter the shop and it was getting popping. It was Wednesday, the midweek mark, and my ladies were booked.

Once the wig was on Jerricka's head I curled her shit fast as fuck while doing the best job that I could. I prayed that I wasn't obvious because I was definitely ready for her to get the fuck up out of my shop. When I was all done, her hair was cute as shit. The fire red thirty inch wig complimented her high yellow skin tone and the flawless natural hairline made that shit seem like it was growing straight out of her scalp. I curled the tresses and combed it out in a loose wave and Jerricka was about to be the baddest bitch at whatever event she attended. As she admired herself in the mirror, I looked down at her with a faint smile on my face.

"This shit is so dope!" Jerricka celebrated. "What's your phone number? I have to send you a tip. Do you have ApplePay?"

"Oh no, it's okay. I'm just happy that I could slay you for your event," I replied.

One thing I wasn't going to do was give this lady my phone number. That was another mental note, to get a business cell phone. We had a landline but clearly that wasn't going to be enough. I was new to this shit and learning as I went and I didn't need to be losing out on tips just because I didn't want to give out my actual phone number.

"No girl, stop playing. I gotta tip you because I appreciate your services and I always tip my people," she insisted.

"I actually don't have ApplePay setup on my phone so it's all good. Thank you for coming out and supporting me and my shop. If you would like to tip, spread the word about me to your friends," I encouraged, pulling my cape from around her neck.

"Or you don't want me to have your number because then I can put two and two together that your number is 813-555-2443 and you was fucking my nigga?!"

Jerricka said that shit so loud that the entire shop got quiet and all eyes darted in our direction. *Here we go, now I'm about to be the ghetto entertainment at my own shop that I preached to these ladies would remain drama free.* I thought to myself. My words might have been caught in my throat but I was still ready just in case this bitch tried to get froggy.

"Ma'am, I'm going to have to ask you to leave," Beast's big ass maneuvered his way between us. It didn't make no sense how quick he could move.

"Now you quiet? Can't say shit and you got a nigga trying to put his hands on me?" Jerricka screeched, her voice cracking with every word.

"Look, I didn't know about you when I met Tazz and as soon as I found out about you and them kids, I left his ass alone."

"Bitch you fuckin' lying! He shot his last music video here, you was shaking your ass all around him and you expect me to believe y'all not fucking?"

"Believe what you want but that's the truth. I got a nigga and it definitely ain't Tazz. I was in the video because Tazz paid me," I shrugged. "You're standing here wasting all of your energy on me when you should be confronting Tazz. *He* is the one that did you dirty. Instead, you down here booking priority appointments to get your hair done. You do nails so I'm positive you knew what to do to get in here without me canceling your appointment. We all know how that shit works. You spent the three hundred dollar priority fee plus the wash, dry, and install fee just to get in here and try to get my phone number. You're too pretty to let that nigga have you going out sad like this, sis."

The other ladies in the shop started snapping their fingers and I heard a few yell out the words "preach" but I guess my words didn't resonate with Jerricka because that bitch lunged at me and as a reflex, I swung, catching her in the jaw. Beast scooped her up and carried her out of the shop while she screamed obscenities. "Just put her down by her car, Beast," I yelled from the front door. Half of the shop watched as she was planted on the ground next to her car. I was irritated as hell now because this was not the example I wanted to set for my stylists.

"And that's how the fuck you clear a bitch!" I heard one of the ladies cackle and they shared laughs and slapped high fives. Me, on the other hand, I went into my office to have a moment to myself because Jerricka had me swinging on her and I was already three dicks removed from Tazz and never planned on going back.

The rest of the day at the lounge was uneventful between Dro bringing me lunch and a smoothie around noon. Then one of the clients that was in the shop recorded the altercation between me and Jerricka and posted it on Facebook so it was being shared around town. I immediately called her and asked her to take it down but I'm sure others already saved it. My last client of the day canceled and I was actually able to head to the back to get my shit together early so I could leave when the last stylist was finished. While on my iMac ordering a business cell phone, a private phone call came through. Although I knew it was Tazz, I decided to answer anyways to curse him the fuck out.

"Tazz, I know this yo simple ass calling me private. It's my fault for doing that music video for you. My nigga was right, I need to stop acting like he ain't got it because now your dumb ass wife pulling up to my shop talking to me like I was the side bitch. Nigga! I never fucking knew about her."

"Chill Yola, she only did that shit because we are getting a divorce. She been found out about you, that bitch finds out about every female I stick my dick in. Jerricka is like the FBI and..."

"Well, I don't give a fuck about you or her. Tell her if she comes up here again, it's gone be a fuckin' problem," I cut him off.

"I know, I just called to apologize and tell you that Jerricka won't be a problem because I threatened to fight her for custody of my kids if she keeps pulling nutty shit. That video of her acting a fool in your shop is already saved and ready for court, she knows how I'm coming."

"Good, now you and her go be nutty together and leave me the fuck out of it," I hung up on his ass.

Everything about today annoyed me and I hated that I agreed to go out of the way to get Dro's favorite wings today of all days but I did that shit. When Dro brought me lunch I was pleasantly surprised that Beast didn't tell him what went on at the shop first thing in the morning. After grabbing the wings, we stopped at Publix to grab a bottle of wine. I just wanted to soak in that big pretty tub and admire myself in the mirror while I rid myself of the negative thoughts. Week one in business hit a ghetto high note.

Stepping out of the bathroom I realized that Dro was already home, stripping out of his outside clothes. When he walked over to me to plant a kiss on my lips, I could taste the lemon pepper on his breath so I knew he already ate before coming upstairs. He showered, handled his hygiene, and returned to the bedroom where I had *Jackie Brown* waiting for him on the tv, a deal was a deal. Dro watched the movie while I updated my booking website. I was done with priority bookings altogether. These hoes wasn't about to catch me slipping like that again.

"Why you so quiet, bae?" Dro pried, squeezing my thigh through my silk robe.

"Nothing, just thinking about how I would kill you if a bitch ever comes to me as a woman," I confessed, he asked so I was telling.

"Man, don't bring that negativity to the bedroom. Beast told me that nigga's wife was about to put them paws on ya ass now you in here tripping on me," Dro laughed.

"Yeah right," I rolled my eyes and laughed a little. Even when I wasn't in a good mood, Dro's mouth always seemed to fix it, verbally or sexually. "Since Beast is out here telling my business, he should've told you that I had to catch that bitch in the jaw. If Beast wasn't there I definitely would've had to kick off my Gucci slides to tap that ass if she wanted to get froggy."

"You need to stop working and give me some jits. Hoes pulling up to your shop and shit. Ion like it. I thought my nigga Beast was getting an easy job but he gotta protect you more than he ever had to protect me. Plus you can run that shit from home. You don't actually have to be in there taking random clients and shit. If you don't want to stop doing what you love, change your policies and only accept appointments from your regular clients."

"I'll think about it." I rolled my eyes as Dro's phone rang, ending the conversation. His eyes narrowed in on the screen before he answered the phone.

"¿Qué pasa tío? (What's up uncle?)"

I sat up in the bed and eased on top of Dro while fumbling with the hem of his boxers. There was something about him speaking Spanish that did it for me every time. Before I could get my favorite freckled tool out Dro grabbed my hips and eased me off of him.

"Damn, I have been looking for her but I had no idea she made her way to Mexico. I'm going down there as soon as I can."

"Nosotros vamos a superar esto. (We are going to get through this.)"

Dro ended the call and I understood that something was wrong because of his change in body language. Plus he thoroughly enjoyed the thrill of me sucking his dick while he was on the phone. "Is everything okay?"

"Priscilla's dead, they are saying that she overdosed on fentanyl."

CHAPTER 11

Dro

"This shit is strictly for business and appearances only. These are my folks and I do business with them but I ain't grow up surrounded by them so you know the bond is kind of different. We really ain't start forming a bond until I turned eighteen and started you know, doing my thing. Maceo was the only one I really had that true familial bond with because he moved to Tampa when I turned eighteen and we were thick as thieves," I informed Yola as we pulled in front of my grandfather's house in the middle of Mexico.

"I know you keep saying that you are okay but are you really?" Yola offered me a sympathetic smile.

"I'm straight. I just wanted to set the tone."

She was beautiful as fuck in the black wrap dress with her hair pulled up into a sleek bun. Squeezing Yola's hand for reassurance, she flashed me a faint smile. I loved the fuck out of this girl. She probably would've much rather be anywhere but here, around a bunch of motha fuckas mourning the bitch who kidnapped her in an attempt to extort money for drugs from me. Yet here she stood, pretty.

I made this trip monthly to chop it up with my Uncle Macario but this time was different. We just left my mother's funeral and now our immediate family was gathering for the repast. Truthfully, I was indifferent about Priscilla's death. I planned to kill the bitch myself but I guess the drugs got to her first. When I arrived at the rehab the nurses informed me that Priscilla had taken off a few minutes before I pulled up.

After watching the devastation that Priscilla's death caused my Uncle Macario, I couldn't bring myself to tell him that Priscilla played a hand in Maceo's demise. He lost his son last year and now we were burying his sister, that was some terrible shit to swallow.

Papá wasn't doing so well either, Priscilla was his only girl and watching them mourn her broke my heart, but the death was expected. Now I was faced with a secret that I wasn't sure what to do with since Priscilla was dead. Initially, I planned to find Priscilla and take her to my uncle and grandfather so she could answer for what she did to Maceo. Now that she was dead, maybe I would just let sleeping dogs lie. Exposing the truth would only open old wounds.

"Alejandro," my uncle greeted me in a somber expression. As he walked in my direction, my grandfather Hector was right behind him.

"Hey unc and Papá, this is my girl Yola. Yola, this is my Uncle Macario and my grandfather Hector," I made the introductions.

"Ella es una hermosa mujer negra," Papá stated, with a mug on his face.

"What the fuck did he just say?" Yola snapped her neck in my direction, forcing me to laugh.

"Relax, bae. Ella es una hermosa mujer negra means she is a beautiful black woman."

A regretful expression washed over Yola's face as her eyes darted towards my grandfather. "I'm so sorry, I thought I heard *nigger* and you were looking so mean," she cringed apologetically.

"No never," he assured her with that same mug on his face.

"Excuse my father, his facial expression hasn't changed since my mother passed away. Be thankful you didn't have to grow up with him as your parent. I never knew whether he was in a good mood or a bad mood when I approached him," Uncle Macario interjected with a hearty laugh and a weak ass joke.

Forcing a fake smile on my face, I just wanted to get this shit over with. I didn't attend funerals and if she wasn't my mother, I wouldn't even be in Mexico. Priscilla gave me life but she also put my safety and business in jeopardy more times than I even realized. I was racking my brain attempting to find out how the fuck she even made it to Mexico because the last time I saw her, she claimed to be flat broke and I left her in that rehab with no money or phone.

"We love Dro and would never disrespect any woman that he has fallen in love with. If he has brought you to meet us, I know that this must be serious," Uncle Macario's voice interrupted my wandering thoughts.

"Yeah, we are serious. This is the love of my life, soulmate, and all that shit," I professed. "She's going to be my wife sooner rather than later."

"Bueno (good), I like her. She's feisty and wasn't even fearful of me when she thought I was disrespecting her," my grandfather expressed, slowly approaching Yola with a grip on his cane.

"Papá, you need to be in your wheelchair."

"Fuck you and the chair, Macario. If you bring it up again, I'll put a bullet in your spine so you can be in the chair. ¿Comprender?"

"I'm going to get a drink and if you fall today, someone else can pick your violent ass up," Uncle Macario shook his head and walked towards the kitchen where bottles of liquor were lined up.

Papá wrapped his free arm around Yola and led her towards the sliding glass door that led to the backyard. He went around introducing Yola as his feisty new granddaughter-in-law and they hit it off, laughing and joking for the duration of the repast. After Yola forced me to eat without an appetite, Uncle Macario summoned me to the office in his home. It was the middle of July and we had our monthly meeting on the third of the month so I wasn't sure what the fuck he wanted to discuss right now. I was currently engaged in a few separate internal debates regarding my personal life, so I couldn't handle shit else.

He bent down and lifted the white crystal metal urn that housed my mother's ashes. *My mother.* That was the first time that I referred to Priscilla as my mother in a very long time. Even though I didn't say the shit aloud, it still shook me a little. Standing in the room with Uncle Macario and Priscilla's ashes was the most uncomfortable experience that I ever endured in my life. I felt sorrow for her soul, but Priscilla got what was coming to her, and I couldn't muster up any tears and there was only a sliver of sympathy in my heart.

"Although our relationship with Priscilla was strained because of her terrible choice in drugs and men, she was still my sister. Every year, we had Priscilla update her will... we knew the drugs would lead to her demise and that's exactly why we wouldn't support her financially.

However, her last wishes were to be cremated and given to you," he lamented before closing his eyes, grief all over his face as he gently tapped the urn. "Sis, I just wish that you would've gotten clean."

"I appreciate you for everything you did for her while she was here and looking out for me as well," I expressed before the door burst open and Yaritza, Macario's wife, barged into the room.

"Papá is dancing with Yola! You guys have to come see it, I swear I even saw that man crack a smirk," Yaritza burst with excitement. We rushed out of Macario's office and I was thankful for the distraction because I wasn't trying to get all sentimental with him in that office. I was already looking Uncle Macario in his eyes, knowing that he was mourning the person who was partially to blame for Maceo's death.

When we entered the backyard, Cardi B's *I Like It* blared through the speakers as my Papá performed his moves the best he could without his cane while Yola swayed her hips to the beat. Papá did a little two step matching Yola's motions with his hands swaying in front of him slowly. Throughout my entire life, Papá always had that same mean mug on his face but he had a slight smile as he moved to the fast-paced rhythm.

"You better watch out, Papá might take your woman," Uncle Macario laughed, pulling his wife onto the floor. Yaritza had on a black and blue flowy dress that she gripped to whine her hips to the beat as Macario eased up to grip her stomach from behind. Personally, they were a lil old for the show they were putting on but who was I to judge? I knew that would be me and Yola in thirty years.

"Nieto." Papá called out to me and motioned me over to him.

"If you were any other man, I would've had to pull out my nine and end the party for trying to dance with my woman," I explained, pulling Yola closer to me. He waved me off as one of my cousins passed him his cane.

"From now on, you bring her back with you when you come for your monthly visits. I love her spunk. Outside of your grandmother, Yola is the only other person to ever have the cajónes to stand up to me. That's why I married your grandmother and gave her three children. If you weren't my grandson, I would definitely steal her from under you. Treat her right, marry her, and give her all the babies she desires. Now that I lost my wife and one of my children, I regret not having more," he panted and took a moment to catch his breath. "I am out of breath and need to sit my ass down."

"Oop," Yola cackled, sticking her tongue out as he wobbled over to a chair with the help of my other uncle, Enrique. "See, that means you better treat me right, I'd hate to have to cheat back with your grandfather."

"Oh you think that shit funny," I grilled her.

Yola gripped my hand and pulled me to the middle of the dance floor. *Tití Me Preguntó* by Bad Bunny was playing and Yola quickly became the life of the party like she always was. This repast turned into a real celebration and the tears were void as the hips swayed to the upbeat music. When it was time for my family to bury me, this was exactly how I wanted to look down and see them.

The next day we were up bright and early, headed to Isla Holbox beach. It was one of the quieter beaches with less tourists. Yola's hand was gripped tightly in one hand and the urn that contained Priscilla's ashes in the other as we trekked along the water. We were silent on the ride over and for the few minutes it took us to walk to the water. Her flowy dress flapped away in the wind with each step we took. Taking a deep breath, I finally decided to express the various thoughts that were swirling around in my head.

"I chose to spread her ashes in the ocean because this was one of her favorite spots to hang. When she used to lock Xan in the room and leave him at the house, she would take me to the beach to snort a lil blow and soak up some sun I guess," I laughed. "That was her shit, back then, I used to think the beach just put her mind at ease because she would always relax and be a lot less snappy when we were at the beach. Now that I'm older, I know that Priscilla used to be high as fuck with my non-swimming ass. Sometimes I think about the fact that I'm only alive by the grace of God because it wasn't by the protection of either of my parents."

Yola yanked on my arm and pulled us both down so we were sitting in the sand. She wrapped her arms around me and I allowed myself to be vulnerable as I melted into her embrace. Her arms pulled me in tighter and she slightly moved from side to side. I needed this shit more than I could've ever imagined. This hug was reminiscent of the hug Mama Nadia gave me when she found out Priscilla left me at home with no supervision for months. Just a bus pass and money for groceries.

"Shit, I know my pops is probably in prison losing his mind. Although Priscilla wasn't shit, he loved the coke head bitch," I stated, standing to my feet. Pulling the top off the urn, I gently dumped the contents into the water and watched them spread in all directions.

"Ion think I can ever swim at the beach again," Yola commented with her face scrunched up once the deed was done.

"Shit I might like that idea because you like to go with them lil ass bikinis on showing my shit off to the world," I agreed with her. "Come on, let's go grab something to eat."

I gripped Yola's hand and we went back to the car in search of food. We wound up at Las Panchas, a little outdoor Mexican seafood restaurant. Since my baby loved shellfish, I knew this spot would be right up her alley. We ate the grilled lobster and tasted a few of their signature cocktails. Watching Yola turn into her usual goofy self over drinks was enough to boost my spirits. I dreaded this trip but I was so happy that I took it with Yola and got to spend some time alone with her.

"Would you guys like anything for dessert?" Our server questioned.

"Nah, dessert is between her legs," I replied, placing a few bills on the table before standing up. Yola's fine ass blushed on the entire ride to the hotel but she already knew what time it was.

CHAPTER 12

Alexander "Big Xan" King Sr.
Two Months Later

Holding onto the five by seven photograph of me and Priscilla on our wedding day, I couldn't believe the shit that my wife pulled. When I met and fell in love with Priscilla I thought I found my ride or die, the woman that would always have my back and be by my side.

"How did we end up here?" I mumbled to myself.

We used to party, smoke, and drink together. Priscilla introduced me to her brother Macario and I was able to start making some real money. I thought that Priscilla was really down for a nigga and that's why I left Nadia and married her ass. To find out that Priscilla was fucking other niggas didn't surprise me. I was on the bench for twenty years, I expected that shit. However, it was the acts committed against Dro and Xan that I could not forgive.

Two days after I received the unexpected visit from Dro and Xan, Frank Russo came to visit me next. We hadn't spoken since he came to tell me about the incident he had with Dro and Xan. Although he was furious, Frank knew that he didn't want to go to war with the Leyva Cartel so he had to hold that L and stay the fuck away from Dro and Xan. Learning that Priscilla was on drugs, I still couldn't believe that she was that far gone until that meeting. Every time I thought about that shit, my stomach churned.

"*Wassup Frank? Everything good?*" I questioned, taking a seat across from him.

"*Not at all. What is this I heard from my son Walter? He said that you are no longer willing to offer him protection while he is fighting for an appeal.*"

"*Yeah man, after learning what he's really in here for, I can't be cool with that shit. I thought he was just a random geeky mufucka in here on cyber crimes or something. You ain't tell me your boy was a pedophile," I grumbled.

"I can understand your apprehension about extending protection to him but we have run into another issue. Your wife paid me a visit yesterday."

"What?" I gritted my teeth, leaning in because if he said some shit I didn't like, I was going to beat his ass and kick my feet up in solitary confinement for a minute.

"Relax," Frank threw his hands up in surrender. "Priscilla came to me asking for help and making some wild accusations. You see, my daughter and her mom were leaving their home a few days ago when they were snatched up by a gang of black men in ski masks and pulled into a truck for a few minutes before they were shoved back out. The men drove for like thirty seconds then said it was a prank before kicking them out of the car. I had to hear about it for the whole fucking day. I had no idea who did it and we checked the cameras from her home but the plates on the trucks were blacked out. According to Priscilla, it was your son Dro. Do you know this to be true?"

"Nah, my son knows the rules of the game, he wouldn't do no shit like that to a woman and child. What reason would he have to harm your wife and child?"

"That's what I asked Priscilla but she couldn't give me an answer. I just wanted to come to you, man to man to let you know that your wife is in bad shape and I helped her across the border. And I will offer her protection from whoever is after her but I need you to look out for my son," he posed a partnership.

"No can do," I shrugged because after hearing this shit, Priscilla was dead to me. She was really willing to sacrifice our son instead of accepting responsibility for her own bullshit.

"Are you sure you want to decline this offer? You can watch out for my fucked up loved one and I can look out for yours. If not, my men are already en route to Mexico which is where she requested we take her and they will leave her at the border with the little money I already gave her and that is it."

"Shit, we are on the road for divorce anyways. Priscilla is no longer my problem," I informed him.

"Oh, I had no idea. My apologies for even bothering you about this matter," Frank nodded then stopped. "I could tell that Priscilla was feigning bad when she popped up at my house. When those drugs have a hold on them, they are *willing to do and say almost anything. However, if it was your son who came near my family, you better make sure I don't find out that it was him."*

"Threatening my son while your defenseless son is in here is crazy," I stood up and offered him a smirk.

Frank stood up and placed his hands in front of him.

"Don't forget that Dro also has the Leyva Cartel behind him," I reminded him before exiting the visitation room.

Thinking back to that day, I already knew where Priscilla would likely go once she made it to Mexico. Her brother and father weren't going to offer her anything but rehab if she showed up on their doorstep in that condition. Mateo would be her only option out there because anyone associated with her family wouldn't help her. I thought back to all of those years ago when Priscilla's family cut her off, she made it seem like they were upset about a deal that went bad between us. Now I was wondering if they cut her off because they knew she was doing coke. Either way it goes, I made the call to Mateo so he could handle her. I couldn't have her running around here putting my boys' lives at risk.

Priscilla told me so many lies over the years that I wasn't sure what to believe when it came to her. It all made sense now that she stopped coming to visit me around the same time she told me Dro cut her off. Priscilla made it clear that she didn't have money to come visit me and I'm sure that's probably when her addiction grew stronger and it became harder to hide it in her appearance. When I was free, I wasn't the most attentive husband or father. After running the streets I usually went to hang with my niggas for a little before I went home. Priscilla and the boys were usually asleep when I made it in. I made it easy as fuck for her to hide her addiction from me. Truth was, I wasn't even looking for shit.

When they say love was blind, I was clearly a living testament of that. Priscilla never told me that she accessed Dro's money before he turned eighteen. When Priscilla brought up the idea of Dro getting into the drug game, she swore that was what he wanted to do. I was against the decision, I wanted him to go to college like Xan and be better than me. At the same time, I knew that a man was going to do what he wanted to do so I decided to help guide him instead of allowing him to jump out there on his own.

I shed a few tears because the journey that I was preparing to embark on was nothing like I imagined when I first got word that the parole board agreed to my release. This was a small secret that I'd been holding onto for the past few weeks because I wanted to surprise Priscilla. I planned to get my life together and live happily ever after with the love of my life while rebuilding the tarnished relationship between me and the boys. Currently, I didn't even know where the fuck I was going once I was released but I knew one thing. The money that I made off of the deal with Frank and Macario was safe and secure. I might have been a fool in love but I already knew not to put all of my eggs in one basket so I'd at least have that to fall back on.

I knew that Dro was trying to settle down and a war was the last thing he needed to be concerned with. Hell, after his girl was kidnapped, a war with the Italian mob would definitely scare her off for good. Despite what my kids thought about me, I loved them and I was going to always have their backs and try my best to make things right.

They called for lunch and I exited my cell on my way to eat some of this nasty ass food. I know you probably think I'd be used to the shit after consuming it for the past fifteen years, but that would never happen. I spent a good portion of my life eating at the finest restaurants, sipping on the best champagne, those memories would never fade. As soon as I got out of this bitch I was going to order the biggest steak and lobster, douse my shit with A1 and butter, and devour that shit just like an untrained nigga fresh out the pen. I ain't have no shame in me.

Standing in line near the cafeteria I felt an unfamiliar feeling that I hadn't felt in a long time. After the way I left that conversation with Frank, I kept my guard up and my senses had that shit on one thousand now, watching my back and my front. Grabbing my tray, I sat with my usual people and slowly ate my food while remaining vigilant. After lunch was over, I was still on my shit but a fight broke out and pandemonium ensued like it did every time mufuckas got to fighting in here.

I moved away from the crowd and got separated from my niggas. Before I knew it, I felt something sharp in my back, the shank was deep inside and whoever was holding it tried to twist it.

"We know that you were behind Priscilla's murder and we want you to rest in hell knowing that somebody is already on their way to your precious Junior too. The Leyva Cartel will never tolerate that type of egregious shit."

With all of the force in me, I flung my head back, knocking the shit out of the young bull with the shank. A guard rushed over to us and pulled the Mexican man away from me as I laid there bleeding the fuck out. I understood the consequences of my actions. I just prayed that Xan wouldn't be harmed as the darkness consumed me.

CHAPTER 13

Dro

Mama Nadia invited me and Xan to brunch with Mr. Phillip and told us to bring Yola and Anya along. I guess she was tired of hearing about them and wanted to meet them in person. With Yola's hand clasped tightly in my grasp, she was checking her makeup in her compact mirror while singing along to the lyrics of *Tomorrow 2*. Xan texted me about fifteen minutes ago letting me know that they were already there and waiting for us. I was always running late so I don't know why he was all stressed in his chest about the shit. I lived an hour out so it took me a minute to get into the city. Leave it to the ladies to choose a brunch spot in the heart of Ybor.

After securing a parking spot, I gripped Yola's hand and led her down the sidewalk on 7th Avenue. We entered the restaurant and I scanned the establishment because the music was loud as fuck and I lowkey felt like I was walking into King's on a Friday night. Since Mama Nadia invited us here, I assumed we were going to partake in a quaint brunch but this shit was lit. Xan stood up and motioned us across the room with a big ass smile on his face and a champagne flute in his hand. My head was still fucked up when we made it to the table as I side eyed Yola.

"You must be Yola," Mrs. Nadia stood to her feet and came around the table to embrace Yola in a hug. "I'm Mrs. Nadia and I've already heard so much about you. I've never heard of Dro dating anyone so this was a pleasant surprise," she gushed over Yola while I was still thinking about knocking her head between the washer and the dryer.

"It's so nice to meet you as well. I've heard good things about you as well. You did your thing raising Xan and Dro has always mentioned how much love he has for you."

"What's wrong Dro?" Mrs. Nadia looked up at me and my eyes darted in Yola's direction.

"Now that I see this shit in action with my own eyes, I see why you always running yo ass to somebody's brunch. So you can day drink and shake yo ass!"

"Boy shut up and sit down," Yola rolled her eyes and pulled me towards the two seats that were waiting for us.

"Nah, I'm dead ass. You was always talking about you going to brunch on Saturday or Sunday and now I see why. I thought you just wanted to have breakfast food with ya friends," I continued talking shit as we claimed our seats. The fact that Mama Nadia and Mr. Phillip were also at the table didn't mean shit to me, they already knew how I was coming.

"Boy you always find something to talk shit about."

"Ain't gone stop either and you ain't going nowhere so stop complaining and get used to it."

"You fuckin' embarrassing me," Yola cringed the moment the words left her mouth. "Shoot, I'm sorry for cursing but Dro knows how to push my buttons. Stop talking mess and introduce me to the other person I don't know at the table before you keep running that mouth."

"Mama Nadia, what you even doing down here?" I ignored Yola's request and addressed her.

"Dro, I'm grown. I come down here with Phillip all of the time and he drives me home. It's usually the highlight of my week," she chuckled.

"Mr. Phillip, you be letting her come down here and participate in this? Y'all should be home knitting or some shit."

"Oh boy, hush," Mama Nadia waved me off. "Since Dro is still being rude, Yola, this is my husband Phillip, Phillip, this is Dro's girlfriend, Yola."

"It's nice to meet you," Mr. Phillip shook her hand and she reciprocated the greeting but I was too busy watching the tipsy girls dancing on each other like it wasn't one o'clock in the afternoon.

"You looking like you wanna be over there with them hoes so maybe yo lil leprechaun ass needs to go over there, I can find a replacement."

LAKIA

"I ain't even going to respond to that shit in front of Mama Nadia but you already know what's up. Don't make me spank you in front of them," I pecked her cheek. "You know I only want you. It's just... I ain't know this is what y'all considered brunch. Mama Nadia, you better keep yo ass in the seat, I'll be damn if you start twerking over the waffles. Yo ass need to be on somebody rocking chair on a porch relaxing."

"Well we need one of y'all to give us some grandbabies if you want us to act like somebody's grandparents. Until then, I'll be having all of the mimosas on Saturday afternoon." Mama Nadia informed me before waving the waitress over. "Can you bring another mango mimosa?"

"Two please," Yola added.

"Actually, make that three," Anya spoke up.

"Of course," the waitress bubbled before taking off.

Me and Yola greeted the rest of the table and were still looking at the menu when the waitress came back.

"So how did you two meet?" Mama Nadia questioned Anya and Xan.

Anya chuckled and took another sip from her glass before looking up at Xan. "You don't want to tell the story?"

"Okay, well one day, I took Brownie to the dog park and she trampled her dog named Rex and broke his leg and the rest is history."

"Awwww, that's a beautiful story to tell your kids when you guys have them," Mama Nadia teared up.

"Alright, that's enough for you," Mr. Phillip shook his head, taking the glass away from Mama Nadia before looking up at me. "See, I don't mind if she gets out there and does her thing with the other ladies, dancing and enjoying herself. But when she starts getting emotional, that's when I cut her off. Nadia is the worst emotional drunk. It's like the tears don't stop once they start."

"Stop telling them my business, Phillip," she nudged his shoulders with a glossy smile before addressing Xan again. "Speaking of Brownie, you are going to have to come pick her up. I have things to do before our anniversary trip and she's been crying for you more and more lately."

"Come on, ma, I need a little more time. I'm still looking for a new house," Xan explained.

"No, it's okay, Brownie can come stay with us as long as we keep a good eye on her and Rex to make sure she isn't too rough with him," Anya assured him. Xan smiled so damn big, you would've thought they were referring to a side baby that Anya decided to accept into her home instead of a damn dog.

"So how did you two meet?" Mama Nadia bubbled, shifting the focus to me and Yola.

Yola damn near spit her drink out, I'm sure she didn't want them to hear how we really met so I sat back and waited to see what bullshit story she could come up with on the fly. "Ummmmm, we were neighbors for a very short period of time," Yola lied.

"Damn, that lie rolled off yo tongue so good. What else you be lying about?" I laughed at her ass. "Nah, we met because I was her neighbor and she banged on the wall to complain about me making too much noise so I had to check her ass. In return, Yola took her snitching ass to the office and got me evicted."

Anya and Xan's eyes widened as they spluttered questions simultaneously.

"So this is who sent the video that got you evicted?"

"He is the one who was fucking some girl all loud in the background of the video?"

Anya was clearly tipsy because I knew her soft spoken ass wouldn't have let the word *fuck* fly out of her mouth in front of Mama Nadia otherwise. Yola sported a look of embarrassment for the first time since I met her, I never thought I would see that shit.

"This is better than *Love & Hip Hop*, please tell me the full story," Mama Nadia urged and I shook my head.

"Hell no, we ain't about to sit here and rehash that entire story. Just know the answer to both of y'all questions is yes and that day led to this and it's a forever thing," I expressed.

"Mommies!" Yola squealed and I glanced up to see Mrs. Latifah and Mrs. Anisha bobbing to the beat as the hostess led them to a table. Their husbands were right behind them and if Yola wouldn't have interrupted their stride, I could tell that they were getting ready to drink these cute ass drinks and cut up in these people's establishment.

Yola made the introductions and pleasantries were exchanged between Mama Nadia and Mr. Philip and the girls' parents. I stood from the table to embrace the women with a hug and dapped the men up before posing a question that was swirling around since Yola called out to them. "Mr. Al and Mr. Tom, y'all be letting them come down here too?"

"Dro hush, clearly you are the only one who never experienced a true brunch vibe," Yola waved me off before waving down the hostess and requesting seating accommodations from the rest of the group.

The hostess pulled another table over to connect to ours and pulled a few chairs for them to sit in as well. They let the patrons day drink, twerk, and rearrange the tables and shit with no hassle. I made a mental note to discuss opening up Kings for brunch on Saturdays with Pinky. Shit looked lucrative. Sitting back, I felt like I really had a family. Although Xan was the only one at this table related to me by blood, I knew everyone else cared about me wholeheartedly.

Standing from my seat and dropping down to one knee, I was happy that I walked around with this ring in my pocket at all times since we got back from Mexico. Initially, I planned to go all the way out with this but the moment just felt right with all of the laughter going around the table as more drinks were brought out.

"Yola," I started, gripping her hand as she squealed with her hand over her mouth. "I love you and you are the woman I want to fill up my big ass house with a bunch of bad ass jits and carry my last name. Shit has been crazy since I floated the idea of us getting married out there. But now seemed like the perfect time since all of our family is here. So Yola, whatchu thinking? You wanna make this shit a forever thing and marry a nigga?" I questioned, popping open the box.

"Although I wasn't looking for love when I met you, I just wanted a new trick. But how could I resist yo fine ass? Yes, I'm going to be Mrs. King! This is my lil leprechaun!" Yola exclaimed, garnering the attention of the entire restaurant. She batted her thick lashes while I slipped the ring onto her finger.

Standing to my feet, I tongued Yola down, hoping she could feel all of the love I had for her. When we finally broke for air, the DJ was playing *Let's Get Married* by Jagged Edge and shouting *congratulations* into the mic. Always the life of the party, Yola started dancing along to the beat as our family came over to congratulate us. I wrapped my arm across Yola's shoulder and allowed her to grind on me. Our family took over the walkway and joined in dancing, all while none of us hadn't ate shit yet. Don't get me wrong, I was happy as fuck to be celebrating this moment but a nigga was hungry as fuck. This restaurant might as well have been a club and I should've ate before I came down here because we hadn't even ordered yet.

CHAPTER 14

Xan

"You look beautiful this morning," I complimented Anya as I entered the house with Rex and Brownie in tow.

We came a long way from their first encounter. Since my mom and Mr. Phillip complained about Brownie at brunch, I had no choice but to bring her to Anya's house. Plus she agreed to help me with her since she could walk Brownie and Rex at the same time. When Rex first saw Brownie, he wasn't with that shit, he ran into Anya's room and stayed there until it was time to go outside. Now they were thick as thieves, laying up under each other near the door throughout the day. I actually caught Brownie taking Rex dog treats on a few occasions, I guess she felt bad watching him limp around with that cast on. He was supposed to be close to being able to take it off and I know my boy couldn't wait for that.

"Thank you," Anya glanced over her shoulder to offer me a flirty smile.

She stood over the stove dressed in a black and blue two piece crop top shorts set with a pair of fuzzy slides on her feet. Anya's legs were so long and slim, her body was curvy in all of the right places, and her outfit fit like a glove. The shit was calling me but I was chilling because I didn't want to make Anya feel too pressured about anything. She was delicate as fuck and I was a patient man.

Outside of Anya looking delectable, the breakfast she was preparing smelled good as fuck in here. When it was time for me to move out, I was going to miss the fuck out of the daily home-cooked meals. I wasn't usually a breakfast man, I mainly grabbed an apple and a cup of coffee and kept it pushing. However, staying with Anya changed that because she was up early cooking breakfast every day.

Even when it was the simple shit like waffles in the toaster and vegan bacon in the air fryer, I appreciated it.

My mama taught me how to cook throughout my teenage years. She always told me that men needed to learn how to cook just as much as women. Being able to cook wasn't about gender, it was about survival. Seeing as though I'd never been in a serious relationship or lived with a woman, my ass would've been down bad if I didn't know how to get in the kitchen and do a lil one-two.

I could actually cook really well but after meeting potential clients, conferring with current clients, and arguing cases all day, the last thing I had energy for when I came home from work was cooking. Prior to me and Anya starting to kick it, I actually used to order some shit off of UberEats to be delivered to the office for me and Preme on our late days. Both Yola and Anya could throw down in the kitchen. That shit wasn't better than my mama's cooking but the food damn sure was comparable. I went into the bathroom to wash my hands then returned to assist Anya in the kitchen. Glancing over Anya's shoulder, I salivated at the sight of the salmon cakes and potatoes cooking on the stove.

"If you want to help speed things up, you can clean and cut the strawberries from the refrigerator. I need a little natural sugar to pair with this," Anya chirped.

"I got you," I confirmed before following her command.

I appreciated Anya for so many reasons. Knowing that I was a pescatarian she always made sure that she cooked something that I could also eat with my diet. By the time I finished slicing the strawberries, Anya was done with the food that she was preparing. We helped each other carry the various dishes filled with food into the dining room and sat down to eat.

"This is like day three of the new house search and you haven't liked any of the properties the realtor has shown you?"

"Nah, I liked a few but I'm taking full advantage and getting the perfect house since Dro ruined the one I thought I was going to grow old in and his ass is footing the bill. I'm going to see a new build house today."

"As you should." Anya giggled and flashed me that perfect smile.

We were sitting next to each other but she was still too far away. Reaching over, I gently slid Anya's chair closer to me and planted a kiss on her lips. Cupping her chin in my hands, I kissed her again as she melted into my chest. We were still at this line but the connection was natural and I was enjoying it. The feeling was beyond any words my brain could formulate. I admired, appreciated, and respected Anya. Everything about her made me want to be her protector and a provider. These emotions were so powerful that I wanted to make sure that everything was perfect for our first time and I had the perfect weekend planned for us on Siesta Key beach.

My phone rang, interrupting the kiss and I pulled away to answer the phone for Kathy, my realtor. "Hello."

"Hi, Alexander. I apologize but my daughter broke her arm and I have to rush her to the hospital. However, the property is available for a self-guided tour if you'd still like to view the home today. If not, I can call you tomorrow to reschedule," she uttered in an exasperated tone.

"No, it's okay. Take care of your daughter, I hope that she is okay. I am fine with the self-guided tour. I have been dragging you around all week."

"Okay, I'll send over the code to the door now. Text me and I'll get back to you," I stated before ending the call.

"You wanna go look at this house with me?" I inquired.

"Of course, I didn't have any plans today," Anya bubbled with excitement. "Since I'm an interior decorator, I love viewing empty homes."

After cleaning up, we were on our way out of the door. The house we were looking at was in southern Hillsborough County in Ruskins. Pulling into the neighborhood, all of the homes were new construction and I could already see me and Anya raising our kids here. Growing old and sitting on the rocking chairs while our grandkids ran around in the front yard.

"This is really nice," Anya gawked over the five bedroom and four bathroom home. It boasted a three car garage, game room, and balcony attached to the owner's suite. We were standing out on the balcony overlooking the neighborhood. Anya's hands cuffed the banister and I eased up behind her, placing my hands on top of hers.

There were moving trucks in front of two of the houses on the block and men moving boxes around while kids ran free in the front yards. That meant people were buying up these homes quickly.

"If it's just really nice, Ion think this is the one for me. I want you to fall in love with it too," I declared.

"I love everything except for the backsplash in the kitchen. Red isn't a color that I would want in my house, especially the kitchen. It's such a violent color," she explained.

"That's an easy fix right?" I pondered, placing my chin into the crook of her neck. She was the perfect height for this position and I sulked it up every time.

"Yeah, it's an easy fix," Anya muttered then paused for a moment as she shuddered in my embrace. "But you can't keep teasing me like this."

She spun around to wrap her arms around my neck, staring up into my eyes with those pretty ass pouty lips poked out. "Watchu mean?"

"I mean, you are always kissing me and saying all of the right things but you haven't gone any further than that and it makes me wonder if something is…"

I already knew where Anya was going with her statement and I wanted to make this weekend special for her but her lustful gaze made my dick hard. Scooping Anya off of her feet, she wrapped her legs around my back, allowing me to squeeze her ass. Anya was light as a feather and all I could think about was all the freaky shit I could do with her.

"Come on, let's go home," I breathed, breaking the kiss.

"No, right now. If we go home, someone is liable to interrupt us again. That kitchen island looks like it's the perfect height," Anya licked her lips.

"Sayless," I placed Anya on her feet and led the way to the requested destination.

Easing Anya up on the kitchen island, I gently massaged her thighs before positioning myself between her legs. Kissing Anya passionately, I felt her hands fumbling with the belt that held up my slacks. "Oh you really want this dick huh?" I cockily pried. Anya bit into her bottom lip and nodded her head yes. My eyes happened to glance behind

LAKIA

Anya's pretty face and the sight of the barrel of a gun sliding through the front door as it cracked open caught my attention. Snatching Anya off of the island, I slapped my hand over her mouth to silence her as I pulled out my gun. Her eyes widened but I placed my index finger over my lips, signaling her to remain silent before I let off two bullets. The bullets pierced the men's skulls and sent their bodies tumbling to the floor.

Anya fidgeted around on the floor with her hands in the prayer position. I stood still with my gun trained on the front door, listening for sounds of anyone else around the house. After about thirty seconds, I knew it must've been clear because I didn't hear shit but the neighbors screaming outside. Gripping Anya's hand, I pulled her off of the floor and gently kissed the top of her head. "It's okay, calm down and breathe."

"What the fuck is going on?" She panicked.

"I don't know but come on, let's go," I directed, pulling out my phone to call Dro but an incoming call from my dad came through.

We hadn't spoken since that day we were searching for Yola. The small voice in the back of my mind told me to answer and I picked up and pressed **0** to accept the call immediately.

"Hello."

"Xan, there is a target on your back, a nigga just tried to take me out and now I'm in the infirmary. Be on your shit, I'm getting out tomorrow and that's all I can say on this phone," he rambled before the call disconnected.

Anya was still on the floor with her arms wrapped around her legs. "Come on, bae," I pulled her up from the floor.

"We can't just leave like nothing ever happened," Anya argued, pulling away from me.

"You wanna stay here and see if more people come?" I questioned but decided to ignore her ass and lifted her off of the ground to carry her to the car.

Anya could be mad at me if she wanted, at least her ass would be alive. I knew a hit when I saw one and I wasn't sure what the fuck was going on, but I wouldn't be here if more men came. Stepping over the dead bodies, I observed their faces and didn't recognize them. They were of Hispanic descent with the letters LC tattooed on their necks. That sent my mind into a deeper rabbit hole because those initials were synonymous with Dro's Uncle Macario's Cartel. Once we stepped outside, we were greeted by two Hillsborough County Sherriff's officers and my plan to get the fuck on went out the window. Dropping my gun on the ground before they could get trigger happy, I began to explain myself.

"We were here doing a self-guided tour when these men came in with their guns out," I explained.

Anya climbed out of my arms and one of the officers came over to kick the gun away from me. As a lawyer, I must advise you to never give a statement, but I already knew I had an immaculate defense because everything I said was true, plus I had observed cameras on the neighbors' houses when I arrived and these fools had their guns out before they entered the home. Of course I was cuffed and placed in the back of one police car and Anya in another. Every time some crazy shit popped off in my life, it never really had anything to do with me, and this time was no different.

I watched as the officers took a few statements from the neighbors, bagged my gun, and we were finally questioned and released after a detective that I was familiar with arrived on scene. As we drove away from the house, Anya was tearfully silent while I shot a 911 text message for Dro to get home. This shit had my mind all over the place.

CHAPTER 15

Anya

My legs shook vigorously the entire ride home and I couldn't get my wandering mind under control until we pulled away from the crime scene. From the moment Xan scooped me off of my feet, everything seemed to be a blur. The police were questioning me but I was too frantic to provide real answers while cuffed in the backseat of a squad car. Throughout my entire life I'd never been in any legal trouble so I didn't know what the hell to do. Xan spoke to me a few times and I didn't respond, just held onto his hand like my life depended on it.

When we pulled up to Dro's house, I finally came out of the fog I was in. Xan led me into the house and I was shocked to see Mrs. Latifah and my mama sitting in the dining room with Yola and an unfamiliar woman. The surprise wore off when I remembered that they were meeting with a wedding planner today.

"Anya baby, are you okay?" Mrs. Latifah questioned the moment her eyes landed on my disheveled appearance.

My mom stood from the table and rushed over to me. The tears were still flowing and only got worse as I attempted to pull myself together to express my feelings. After I couldn't speak, the attention went from me to Xan and they looked like they were ready to pounce on his ass while they drilled him with questions back to back. He didn't have a chance to answer the first question before the next person shot off another one. The chatter wasn't doing shit to get my emotions under control, in fact, it was only making things worse. Dro barged through the door before either of us had the chance to answer any questions from the three women.

"Who the fuck tried to kill you Xan?" Dro snarled, his freckled face red with anger.

"Someone tried to kill you? What the fuck y'all got going on?" My mom snapped at Xan then looked at me, clasping both of my cheeks between her hands. "Anya baby, are you okay?"

I nodded my head rapidly, attempting to assure them that I was fine but I was doing a horrible job.

"That's it! Yola and Anya, get y'all shit together," Mrs. Latifah ordered. "One time is bad luck, the second time is a sign that these aren't the men for you. They got too much going on and your safety is more important than anything else! I was biting my tongue and trying to give them the benefit of the doubt but fuck that! This is the sign you needed to leave them ***the fuck*** alone. Let's go!"

Hearing the blame being placed on Xan and the thought of leaving him at that moment weren't a part of the plan. After what we went through earlier, it made me want to protect Xan just like he did me. Searching hard, I finally found my voice as I continued to hold Xan's hand.

"I'm not going anywhere. What happened wasn't Xan's fault," I argued.

"Who the fuck is that?" Dro pointed his finger at the wedding planner who stood in the dining room watching the entire scene unfold. I'm sure she was attempting to digest this made for tv drama just like the rest of us. Dro's words snapped her back to reality and she quickly began to gather her things.

"That's the wedding planner," Yola informed him. "Yo light bright ass was supposed to be here so we could get your input for the wedding an hour ago."

"I ummm... we can just reschedule," she faltered, walking past the family with a laptop and stack of papers in her hands.

Dro led her out and Xan went to grab me some water. "I'm fine," I declined the water he extended in my direction.

"Look ma," Dro started once he re-entered the dining room. "I know shit seems a lil crazy..."

"A little? Ain't shit little about your mother kidnapping my daughter and now Xan is out with Anya and someone tried to kill them?!" She cut him off.

"Okay, so maybe *little* wasn't the proper term. I know shit has been out of hand but I'm going to handle everything. I put that on me," Dro patted his chest. "I'll sacrifice my life before I allow anyone to harm Yola and Anya."

"Yeah ma, you trippin'," Yola added. "Let me walk y'all out. We will reschedule the meeting with the wedding coordinator and keep y'all posted."

"So you expect us to just leave without even knowing what's going on?" My mom argued.

"Yes mom, we are grown," I clarified for her.

"You grown? Your ass was just two seconds away from a fucking panic attack!" She chastised me.

"And now I'm sipping water and about to go take a shower to ease my mind and probably go to sleep," I accepted the water from Xan and took a sip. "I'm fine, I love you," I planted a kiss on her cheek.

"If anything happens to my girls…" my mama fumed before snatching her purse off of the table to leave.

Me and Yola walked our moms out and the men were engaged in a heated debate once we returned. I still didn't know what exactly was going on but I trusted Xan to keep me safe. Plus the added security features that Dro had on his house were next level so I wasn't concerned about anyone coming here. If they did, they wouldn't have any success entering the home.

"Do you really want to take a shower and nap? There are plenty of rooms here and I don't want you going home by yourself."

"I really do want to take a shower," I informed her.

"Okay, let me show you the guest bedroom that I like the most," Yola advised me before leading me up the stairs.

She stopped at a large linen closet and pulled out a plush cotton towel and rag then grabbed a bottle of her favorite Honey Milk body wash. I could see why her ass didn't want to leave Dro's house. He already had everything laid out for her in this compound. I accepted the towel and rag then trailed Yola to the bedroom in question. Upon entering the room my head swiveled from the decor in the room then back to Yola.

"What is this?" I pondered aloud.

"I already told Dro that you and Rex would need y'all own room for when y'all come over and it's too late for y'all to make the hour drive home and he was down," Yola bubbled.

The room was decorated in lilac, my favorite color, and there was a small dog bed in the corner that was the perfect size for Rex. Sauntering into the bedroom I plopped down on the bed to test it out and it was pillow-top mattress soft.

"I haven't had a chance to decorate the bathroom in here yet because I wasn't planning to tell you about the room until the next time you needed to spend the night. However, the bathroom is clean," she explained, easing onto the bed next to me. "So what the hell happened that had you shook and Dro coming in here like a raging bull?"

Taking a deep breath, I ran the details about what happened to Yola. By the time I was done, she sat there looking just as stuck as I felt. "Damn, Xan pulled out a strap and shot two niggas? I ain't think Xan had that in him. This might sound crazy, but did seeing him in action turn you on a lil?"

"Hell no bitch, I was scared for my fuckin' life and freedom!" I groused.

"Well I'm just saying," Yola batted her lashes. "Knowing that Dro will kill a mufucka to protect me gets the cat wetter than it ever has before."

"My ass was in there crying and shaking. He had to pick me up and carry me out of the damn house. If I'm being honest, all I was thinking about was how we needed to get the fuck away from Dro and Xan as he let off shots. But as I watched him in the back of the police car, all I could think about was losing him because he went to prison for murdering those men and that scared me more than him killing those men while I was in the room with him. Then he held my hand the entire ride home, kissing it periodically while asking me if I was okay and assuring me that he was going to make sure I was safe. I believe Xan when he says he will keep me safe or else I would've ran up out of here with our moms a few minutes ago."

"I definitely understand that. Unfortunately, even if we wanted out, it's too late. Priscilla snatching my ass up taught me that an enemy of my man will target my ass without hesitation and this is probably the safest place to be if some shit is amiss." Yola stood from the bed and planted a kiss on my forehead.

Exhaling deeply, I stood from the bed with my shower essentials and went into the bathroom. That was probably the longest shower I'd ever taken in my life because I did more thinking than showering. When I came out of the bathroom Xan sat on the edge of the bed, worry evident in his appearance because he didn't even see me approaching. I took a shower but my ass didn't even think about what I would wear once I got out.

Xan looked up at me with the towel wrapped around my body and gripped both of my hands before kissing them gently. I couldn't relate to murder making Yola's kitty tingle, but it was the random knuckle kisses and the concern that Xan showed me that got my juices flowing.

"Are you sure you're okay? If you want to go with your parents, I understand but I am going to need you to let two of Dro's men go with you until we figure out what exactly is going on," Xan explained.

"No, I'm where I want to be," I avowed, releasing the grip I had on my towel.

Leaning in to kiss Xan's lips, he accepted my tongue and caved under my weight, allowing us to plop down on the bed. My nerves were in a tizzy but after coming so close to losing my life, I realized that nothing was promised. Xan was who I wanted to be with and like Yola suggested when I was drunk leaving the club a while back, I just needed to stop playing and suck his dick.

Pulling myself off of Xan, I fumbled around with his slacks until his dick was free. Before Xan could protest, I made sure my mouth was wet and slid his dick down my throat. I was nervous until he allowed a low moan to escape his lips as he gently massaged my scalp. Using the tips provided and my previous experience I gripped his dick with both hands and caught a good rhythm sucking his dick.

"Shit, just like that," he encouraged me and I continued until I was out of breath.

When I came up for air, my tongue swirled around the head of his perfect brown dick. I was quite intimidated by its size initially but the noises he made gave me the motivation to keep going. My tongue trailed down his dick until I gave his balls a little love and that must've been all he could take because he pulled me up so fast.

Once I was on my feet, Xan kicked his slacks the rest of the way off and pushed me down onto the bed. He moved so quickly that I didn't have a moment to prepare for the intense amount of pleasure that his long thick tongue provided once it collided with my clit. I hate to admit this shit but he did that little trick where he pulled the hood of my clit back and licked purposefully. As much as I wanted to keep it down I couldn't. It only took a gratifying thirty seconds before I reached my first orgasm.

"Fuck! Xaaaaaaaaaaan!" I moaned out so loud as my back formed a deep arch with my head leaned all the way back.

My hands went to Xan's head as he kept licking, I swear I felt like I was going to lose it but he didn't stop and held me tighter as I attempted to fight him off. He slid his finger inside of me and I swear I thought I perished and transitioned to a permanent state of ecstasy. The way my body tingled was electric and it didn't take long for the second orgasm to take over. This time, I gripped his head and grinded into his face. I couldn't help the way my body reacted if I tried. Yelping his name until the orgasm passed, I was happy that Xan finally ceased his assault on my clit and trailed his tongue up my stomach until his handsome face was adjacent to mine. Xan kissed me so deeply while my legs spread like they had a mind of their own. I gripped the sides of his face while he kissed me with my essence covering his beard and lips. He pulled away from me and peeled off his shirt, exposing the body that I loved to stare at in my spare time.

"Ahhhhhhh," I gasped lowly as Xan slipped his dick inside of me.

All of the years that I remained abstinent were worth it for this moment right here. This shit hurt so good as he spread my walls to fit him and Xan's low grunts confirmed that he was loving it too. The way Xan kissed me while taking his time to stroke my kitty at a loving pace was sending me over the edge. Then I felt his tongue slide down my neck and I knew that I was going to reach my orgasm soon. As if he could read my mind, Xan started going deeper while staring me in my eyes. The love was there, I knew it and decided to profess my feelings through my orgasm.

"I love youuuuuu!" I squealed through my orgasm.

Xan pulled his dick out as soon as the words left my lips and he used his shirt to catch his nut. Collapsing on the bed next to me, Xan pulled me onto his chest and pulled my face up to meet his gaze. "I love you too," he confirmed before emitting a slight chuckle. "I almost nutted as soon as you said that shit. I love you, Anya," he repeated himself.

"I love you too," I expressed before nuzzling my head into Xan's chest. I wanted to go for another round but I was drained and lowkey embarrassed about all of the noise I made. Hopefully Dro and Yola were outside or in the gym or something. When I said I was going to take a nap that wasn't on the agenda but all of that damn crying then the much needed sex, I was fast asleep before I knew it.

CHAPTER 16

Xan

Watching Anya fast asleep on my chest was refreshing but that sex session boosted my spirits with all of this crazy shit going on around us. When Mrs. Latifah and Mrs. Anisha started popping their shit yesterday, I definitely thought Anya was going to run up out of here right behind her mother. If she would have, I couldn't even blame her. She witnessed me murder two men that wouldn't have thought twice about killing the both of us if I didn't look up when I did. I hated to even think about how close I came to losing my life earlier. Two minutes later and I would've been too deep in Anya's pussy to have been aware of my surroundings. My phone vibrated in my pocket and I slid my hand inside to retrieve it.

"Hello," I answered in a low whisper so I wouldn't disturb Anya's slumber.

"Wassup Xan? I just picked up the dogs and pulled up at your mom's crib and she said you told her that we were on the way but she ain't coming with us," Beast explained.

Sighing deeply, I eased myself from under Anya and stepped out of the room. It was eight o'clock in the morning and I wasn't in the mood for this shit. I hadn't even had breakfast yet.

"You think I care that you called my son? I said I'm not going anywhere and you better stop playing before my husband beat yo ass," I heard my mom in the background.

"Please put her on the phone," I requested.

"Xan asked to speak with you," Beast informed her.

"I said I'm not changing my plans. Phillip has been planning our anniversary trip to France for months and we are going."

"I didn't say y'all couldn't go. I just asked you to delay the trip and

LAKIA

come to Dro's house until we can charter y'all a private jet since I couldn't get flights for Dro's men on the flight y'all taking."

"Nope, I'm not taking these damn babysitters either," she refuted before disconnecting the call.

Tightening my fists, I couldn't believe how stubborn my mama was acting. A nigga ain't have time for this bullshit right now. Yesterday, Dro made a call to his Uncle Macario after I told him about the phone call with Big Xan and the men I had to handle, it was clear that the Leyva Cartel was behind the attempt on my life. Unfortunately, Dro was unable to reach Macario or his grandfather to see what was up. Until we could gather the answers we needed, my mother's safety was my responsibility. We still hadn't heard from Big Xan although he claimed today was his release date. I spoke with the lawyer that I referred my father to a while back and he confirmed he was being released, but Big Xan asked him to keep it a secret so he could surprise us. However, the nigga still hadn't turned up yet after that rushed vague phone call from yesterday.

I went back into the bedroom to brush my teeth and take a piss then I was on my way back out of the bedroom headed to my mom's house. On my drive over there I called Dro to inform him of the situation and to see if he had heard from Big Xan. A little over an hour later I pulled up to my mother's home and took a deep breath in preparation for the battle I knew I'd be facing once I made it inside.

Nodding at Kenny, the second man that Dro felt comfortable watching over my mom, I approached the door and was greeted by Beast's face first. My mom was sitting at the counter with a cup of coffee in her hand and her phone to her ear.

"Girl let me call you back, Xan just walked through the door," she rolled her eyes as I approached her.

"Where is Mr. Phillip?" I questioned.

"He's in the back packing his luggage so we can go to the airport," she spoke confidently, placing her hand on her hip. "*I'm* the mother in this situation and there isn't anything that you can say to change my mind and Phillip agrees."

As soon as the words rolled off of my mother's tongue, I heard multiple voices on the porch. Ignoring my mother's attitude I headed towards the door to see what the hell was going on. The door swung open and Kenny looked at me then back to Big Xan. "I know he looks like you but Dro gave me strict orders not to let anyone outside of you and him around your mom," Kenny stated with his gun by his side.

"Tell jit he got five seconds to put that gun away before I take it and shove it down his throat," Big Xan snarled, his eyes trained on Kenny.

I quickly cut in after the instant state of shock wore off, here Big Xan was, free just like he stated the day prior. "It's okay Kenny," I nodded my head.

As Big Xan entered the home, I noticed my mother tense once she laid eyes on him. While Nadia wore a look of bewilderment, my father appeared love struck at the sight of my mother. She was dressed in a pair of PINK joggers and a matching sports bra. I wanted to cover her ass up because it was clear this nigga was salivating over her.

"I got everything packed up," Phillip announced from their bedroom before I saw him wheeling their suitcases down the hallway.

"Who the fuck is this?" Mr. Phillip waved his hands in Big Xan's direction mockingly before continuing his rant. "We told you we don't need any security and we aren't altering our vacation dates. I have been protecting my wife since we met and that won't stop now just because you and Dro got yourselves into some mess. The last thing I'm going to have is some other niggas watching me while on vacation, I might wanna slide your mama to the edge of the beach and do some freaky shit real quick."

I wanted to talk shit about him discussing their sex life with me but I was enjoying watching my father's heart shatter the more he spoke about protecting my mom with the confidence to match. "Phillip, baby, this is Alexander Sr.," she explained, walking over in his direction. Mr. Phillip looked up for the first time and noticed the similarities in our features. "I had no idea he was out of jail, coming here, or anything like that."

"You don't have to explain yourself," he assured her with a kiss to the lips.

"It's nice to meet you," Mr. Phillip came over and shook Big Xan's hands.

LAKIA

"Likewise," he nodded his head.

The door swung open again and Dro barged in talking shit. "Mama Nadia and Mr. Phillip, y'all got me fucked up talking about y'all still going on this vacation. I'll pay for y'all to reschedule and go another time but right now isn't the time."

"I just finished telling your brother I'm not worried about what y'all got going on. I'm going on vacation with my wife and I'll make sure she's safe," Mr. Phillip waved Dro off before turning to my mom. "You ready, baby?"

"Yeah, I'm ready."

"Alright, everybody out. We have a flight to catch and memories to make," Mr. Phillip motioned us towards the door in a shooing motion. Once we all stood on the porch, me and Dro hugged both my mother and Mr. Phillip and watched them get into the car like the disobedient parents they were.

"Raising your parents is definitely harder than raising kids because these motha fuckas don't listen," Dro talked shit as he sparked a blunt in their front yard.

"I know their hotel info so we can just have Beast and Kenny hop on a flight and if those two nasty mufuckas start doing some freaky shit, don't be looking at my mama," I ordered on my way to the truck they rode over there in to retrieve the dogs from the backseat. Dro hit them with some cash and sent them on their way to pack and book a flight to France.

Big Xan hadn't uttered a word since saying *likewise* to Mr. Phillip a few minutes ago. That bitch *karma* was showing out and Big Xan had the nerve to look like his entire world caved in around him. I guess he must've forgotten that he lived a double life for years and eventually left her for the other woman.

CHAPTER 17

Big Xan

Yeah I knew that Nadia remarried but I can't lie, I had a false sense of hope that the shit wasn't that serious and I arrogantly brought my ass over here thinking I could finesse something with her. It was no secret that Dro and Xan weren't feeling me but I figured I could always count on Nadia. However, Nadia glared at me like she was repulsed by my appearance alone. Then she greeted that nigga with a kiss right in front of me, shattering my heart in a million pieces. I suffered the worst type of heartbreak twice this year. First with Priscilla and now with Nadia.

If that wasn't bad enough, I felt like an outsider with my own kids. Watching them embrace Phillip brought me back to reality. I really wasn't there for my boys like I should have been prior to my incarceration and over the last fifteen years, they built their own lives and constructed familial bonds. It was evident that Phillip was a father figure to them, then hearing Xan and Dro refer to them as their parents cut deep. Especially because I was their father and they were calling me Big Xan like the rest of the world.

"For a nigga that just got out of the penitentiary after serving fifteen years, you definitely don't look happy to be home," Dro interrupted my thoughts with his dumb ass statement. I knew for a fact that both of my sons knew why my head was fucked up.

"This nigga ain't picked his face up off of the floor since he saw Mr. Phillip walking down the hallway," Xan shook my head.

"You know, I was wondering why the fuck you was here but thought maybe Xan neglected to tell me that he scooped you up. I know you ain't bring your ass over here thinking that you could weasel your way back into Mama Nadia's heart," Dro laughed. "Nah, Mr. Phillip takes good care of her so that shit dead. I have been to the gun range with him too so let me warn you that his aim is official, don't get that shit twisted because he ain't a street nigga."

"She answered one phone call and you thought you could finesse your way back into her good graces. Ion see why you all stressed in your chest now. You left mama and she upgraded to a lawyer who loves, respects, and protects her," Xan added in while his dogs sniffed around me.

"I ain't gone front, it fucked me up to actually see her with another nigga but I'm straight," I cleared my throat as they passed the blunt back and forth. The urge to smoke was more persistent than ever but I was on papers for the next year and wasn't risking my freedom for shit.

"Alright, Mama Nadia is long gone and we have bigger matters to handle. What the fuck is going on? Why would my uncle or Papá want you dead?" Dro quizzed.

I took a deep breath, unsure about how he would respond to my confession but I decided to spit the shit out. "I had Priscilla killed. I had a hunch that one of my partners in Mexico was her dealer when she was in town. I knew it was a gamble having Mateo tamper with her shit but it was a risk I was willing to take. Unfortunately, Mateo's sister told me some men from the Leyva Cartel picked him up because they found out he was Priscilla's dealer when she was in Mexico. The rest is self-explanatory."

I braced myself just in case Dro decided to get some stress off of his chest with my confession. Taking a long hard pull from his blunt, Dro looked up at me before speaking again. "I'm indifferent," he shrugged. "I planned to deliver her to Uncle Macario when I found her but she never turned up. I've been trying to get up with my uncle and Papá since Xan killed two of their men but he isn't answering the phone. When I spoke with my Uncle Enrique, he said that Macario is out of the country with Papá and they didn't say where they were going. The hit is already in motion and Enrique isn't in the family business, he was a pharmacist running a legit business before he retired so he can't stop shit. So now that *you* killed Priscilla and brought all of this heat to our front door, what's the game plan?"

I could sense the agitation in Dro's voice but I had a contingency plan just in case the Leyva Cartel found out I was the one behind

Priscilla's death. "Well they won't hurt you because you're their family and had nothing to do with it. As for us, clearly they don't give a fuck about our familial connection to you so we all have to play our part. Xan gotta represent Walter Russo so we can have the Italian mob on our side. The way I see it, The Leyva Cartel cannot afford for both of y'all organizations to stop receiving shipments from them at one time. I know they will cave for sure."

"So they would be willing to put their drug supply on the line just to have Xan as a lawyer?"

"Yeah, they still haven't found a lawyer for Walter. Now that I know what he was charged with, I could understand why. That Frank motha fucka has dirt on the rest of the family and is threatening to talk if he doesn't get out. Their freedom is on the line and Frank won't harm his son so they are willing to do whatever. I orchestrated the connection between the Russo Mob and the Leyva Cartel from behind bars with the help of Priscilla so I can deal with the Russo Mob."

"Great plan, wrong nigga. I ain't getting Walter out of prison," Xan spoke with finality. He swaggered over to his Benz with the dogs trailing behind him, leaving me and Dro to watch him drive off.

"Xan ain't gone do that shit and Ion wanna work with them nasty motha fuckas either. Plus I kind of almost kidnapped Frank's daughter and ex-girl."

"I know and that's why I decided that Priscilla was too dangerous to run the streets. She went to Frank Russo and told him that you kidnapped his daughter."

"So why the fuck do you think we could work together?" Dro vexed.

"Frank said that Priscilla was sober and feigning bad when she landed on his doorstep and I assured him that you wouldn't do anything like that."

"You should've consulted me before doing all this dumb shit because I already had plans in motion for Priscilla and now the shit is all fucked up," Dro chastised me before walking to his Range Rover. "Do you need a ride?" He paused before entering his truck.

"That would be nice. I just need you to drop me off at Tremaine's house in South Tampa. That's where I'm paroled to."

"Bet... and stay the fuck away from Mama Nadia," he ordered as I climbed into the truck.

"She ain't checking for me and I get it," I threw my hands up in surrender.

"You better, me and Xan love Mr. Phillip and I'd let him smoke you about Mama Nadia," Dro shrugged harshly. I had a lot of making up to do and I planned to do just that. Tremaine had the money I made from the deal with the Russo Mob and Leyva Cartel put up for me. Once I had that, I could get back on my feet and begin the process of rebuilding the relationship with my boys. Before I could even think about rebuilding that relationship, I had to squash this beef with the Leyvas.

CHAPTER 18

Yola

After everything popped off with Xan and Anya yesterday, Dro let us know that we were confined to his house or my shop and he had two new men with us at all times until further notice. On the average day, I would've put up a big fight about this shit because I liked to come as I pleased and I didn't know these new niggas like this. I was already used to Beast tailing me but now I had two unfamiliar men to keep me company, no bueno. The shit was annoying as fuck and I couldn't wait until they worked out whatever mess they were in with Dro's family. I couldn't believe that shit turned into this because I loved his maternal side of the family when we met. They all seemed extremely sweet and welcomed me with open arms.

It was Sunday and the shop was closed so we were grabbing lunch at Gyros while we were in the city before heading home. "Damn, I thought we would be in and out since the drive thru line was so long. It's just as bad in here," Dro commented, taking probably the tenth spot in line. "We could've ordered our shit to go from Peabody's and been on our way but naw, you wanted to come to Gyros," Dro talked shit while pulling me back into his arms. He nuzzled his chin into the crook of my neck tickling me with that facial hair before planting a kiss on my neck.

"No, I wanted Gyros," I argued. The line was long as hell and I had to pee so I excused myself and went to the bathroom. After relieving my bladder, I washed my hands and exited the bathroom with my face buried in my phone scrolling through my TikTok feed. My ass was slacking bad as fuck lately and I needed to get back on my social media shit. I went from posting three times a day to three times a week since I opened the shop. Things were just so fast paced at the shop that it was difficult to remember to record content while I was in the process of doing hair. As deep as I was in my thoughts, my neck snapped up quick as fuck when I noticed a bitch invading Dro's space.

"Hey handsome, we should link when ya not busy ya know," she flirted. I scanned her body and the brown skinned bitch was beautiful but she didn't know how to play the game. Coming on that strong would never entice a nigga with money to splurge on you long term. The most you'd do was flash a lil smile and let them come to you.

"Nah, I'm sorry. I have a fiancée," Dro's dumb ass informed her while stepping back. Storming over, I slapped Dro across the back of his head and he flinched before glaring at me. "What the fuck you do that for?" He questioned. Too pissed to respond, I scowled at him with my eyebrows furrowed before folding my arms across my chest underneath my titties. Storming out of Gyros with my lip poked out and jaw clenched so hard, I thought it would shatter. Dro's annoying ass was right on my trail.

"What the fuck wrong with your crazy ass?" Dro badgered.

"Saying sorry means you would fuck if you weren't with in a relationship with me and nigga, Ion wanna hear that bullshit. It should've been, 'no, I got a woman.' Hard motha fucking stop with no room for error, block head ass nigga. Just like you told me all of these niggas need to be ugly and broke, these hoes need to be ugly with ran through pussies to you!" I snapped at him, ready to take his head off if he said some shit I didn't like.

Sighing deeply, Dro snatched my arm and practically drug me back inside of Gyros.

"Nigga, let me go. I'm not hungry anymore. I just wanna go home!" I argued, fighting to free myself from his hold but it's obvious Dro was the stronger one in our relationship. My feet worked overtime to keep up with his angered pace until we were standing in front of the woman that was smiling in Dro's face a few minutes prior.

"Ayeeee, I wouldn't fuck you with a junkie's dick, ma. Don't ever approach me like that again, I'm happily engaged," Dro spat, lifting my hand so she could see the big ass rock on my finger.

"Ummm, okay," the woman stammered, taking a step back.

"Now you doing too fucking much," I huffed, yanking my wrist out of his grasp. Arms folded across my chest again, I was fuming on my way out of Gyros. My steps didn't stop until I was standing next to Dro's Range Rover.

"What the fuck you want from me, Yola? You ain't like the way that I rejected her earlier and now I made that shit clear. You said you didn't want any room for error and I didn't leave any," his dumb ass clarified.

"Just take me home like I said like five minutes ago!" I yelled.

"Sayless," Dro grumbled as he opened the door to my car.

We drove home in silence. He was clearly pissed and I was equally as infuriated. When we got home, Xan and Anya were in the gym and we bypassed them.

"What happened to the Gyros?" Anya questioned.

"Ask Dro's dumb ass," I retorted on our way to the bedroom.

"We didn't get food and Yola gave me a fucking headache and because of the dumb ass shit that happened, we left before we got food."

Once inside of the bedroom Dro peeled out of his shirt while I plopped down on the bed. There was still a bottle of D'Usse on the dresser from Dro's lazy ass and I pulled the cap off to take a little to the head in an attempt to ease my mind. He snatched it from my lips after I took three long swigs. "What the fuck is your problem?" He questioned in a calm tone this time. "You said you didn't want me to leave room for error when rejecting these bitches and I was trying to give you that. Then you're still mad so I need you to help me understand for real."

"But that girl ain't deserve that shit and you got me looking like an insecure ass bitch out here. I'm far from insecure, Dro! I know another bitch could never have you like I do."

"Well then fucking act like it!" Dro barked on me before pausing to exhale deeply.

"Fucking make me!" I commanded, dragging out each syllable in the words, ready to rip Dro's head off if he said some shit I didn't like.

His hands grasped my waist and he pulled the joggers I was wearing down around my ankles before turning me around over the bed. He slapped my ass and as much as I wanted to remain mad and not cave in to his nasty ass, I couldn't. A low moan escaped my lips and he slapped my ass again a little harder that time. Dro spun me back around with his hand gripped firmly around my neck as he pushed me down onto the bed.

Gripping my knees he forced my legs apart with just the right amount of force that I could feel his frustrations without him actually hurting me. Dro was already stripped down to his boxers, making it easy for him to whip his dick out and stick it inside of me.

"You wanted me to make you act like you know I only want you, right? That's what the fuck you said?" Dro questioned, gripping my neck to choke me slightly. He roughly thrust inside of me while pulling me up by my neck to meet his lips. The deep forceful kisses that Dro blessed me with almost took my breath away. He broke the kiss and squeezed my neck harder as he drilled inside of me.

"Fuck! I'm about to cum!" I panted.

"Cum on this dick for me with yo pretty mean ass!" Dro coaxed, releasing the grip he had on my neck to play with my clit and grip my hip with the other hand. He was administering those long deep rough strokes that drove me crazy. My eyes rolled to the back of my head and I felt my body quaking as I screamed. "Drooooo!"

He pulled out and I felt his nut spill onto my stomach. My body relaxed on the bed when I heard him go into the bathroom to retrieve a warm rag. "If you wanted to start an argument so I could fuck you all rough and shit, you could've just said that."

"No, you really pissed me off," I expressed, looking up at him.

"If you feel like you handled that shit appropriately earlier then I clearly didn't do a good job making you get some act right," he grinned, tossing the soiled rag into the dirty clothes basket before pulling me up from the bed. I barely had a moment to catch my breath or respond before Dro bent me across the bed and stuffed his dick in me from the back.

We went at it for another two rounds, drinking D'Usse in between until we fell asleep. The next morning I woke up naked and sweaty. We never left the room to eat and drunk half the bottle of D'Usse. Jumping from the bed as I felt my stomach churn, I sprinted into the bathroom and vomited into the toilet. It seemed to be endless and I couldn't wait for the shit to stop.

"Awwwww shit, it all makes sense now." Dro entered the bathroom rubbing his hands together excitedly. I looked up at him, feeling like death and despair. "That pussy is always super gushy but last night, a nigga felt like he was swimming, it was so wet. Plus last night, I thought you was really going to try to fight a nigga. Don't get me wrong, shit talking is our love language but you were mad as hell about some petty shit yesterday. No matter how mad you are, yo ass gone eat. Now you throwing up after that fuckin' tantrum you threw in Gyros. I already know what's up and you do too."

I was drained from vomiting and couldn't gather the strength to process what he was insinuating for real. He rushed over and flushed the toilet and helped me over to the sink where he wet a rag to place on my forehead.

"Now isn't the time for us to have a baby," I exhaled deeply.

"Yeah but only because of this shit between Big Xan and Macario," he fumed, gently rubbing his hands through his beard like he always did when he was in deep thought. "I can't even celebrate like I want to because of the fucking targets on Xan and Big Xan's backs. When it's all said and done, that shit trickles down to everyone around me."

Dro exited the bathroom while I was brushing my teeth and by the time I returned to the bedroom his phone and keys were gone. I went downstairs to search for him and found the house empty besides Anya and Xan. Taking a deep breath, I was pissed off that he took off that fast. I placed a call to his phone and was met with the voicemail. After vomiting, I didn't have energy for anything else except the shower and going back to sleep. Realizing that I was possibly pregnant and having Dro take off without a word shortly afterwards wasn't anywhere in my life plans, yet here I was. Looking up at the ceiling, I rolled my eyes and went back to sleep pissed off.

CHAPTER 19

Dro

The most toxic bullshit in the world can be family if you are born into a fucked up one. I was born to a coke head and a drug dealer who both had more pressing matters than raising me. My own mother brought her coked out boyfriend to rob me and I wound up with two bullet holes to the chest. I came to the family to ask for permission to end her life and was told no. These motha fuckas told me she was still my mother, my Papá's daughter, my uncle's sister, and they wanted to give her a chance to get clean. **Fuck family** if that's how they were going to move. The only family I really needed or cared for was Xan and Mama Nadia. Now I had Yola to protect and a baby on the way. Plus my brother, the only motha fucka that always had my back, was a walking target because of a woman who never truly cared for me the way that I deserved.

I was on a private jet headed straight to the source to see what type of understanding we could come to. If not, I'd have to pull my people together and go to war with the Leyva Cartel. Allowing anyone to harm Xan or Mama Nadia wasn't even an option. Once we landed, I was on the way to my grandfather's house. If they still weren't back from where ever the fuck they went, I was prepared to wait for their return. I wasn't leaving Mexico until this issue was resolved or I initiated a war, the outcome was completely dependent on my maternal family.

As I sped through the streets of Mexico, I checked in with Beast to make sure that Mama Nadia and Phillip were still straight and they were. The only reason I didn't put up a real fight about them taking this vacation was because it was probably better for them to get the fuck away from Florida while we sorted shit out. Although the man who shanked my father in prison only mentioned a target being placed on Big Xan and Xan's back, I didn't put shit past my uncle. The Leyva Cartel had a ruthless reputation for a plethora of reasons.

Pulling into the rounded driveway of my grandfather's home, I noticed a few unfamiliar cars in the driveway. Making sure my shit was tucked, I exited the car and immediately observed the bikini clad women holding Corona's scattered about the front of the house. Some music by Bad Bunny blared through the backyard and I shook my head. It appeared as if Uncle Macario and Papá were out of town and Uncle Enrique was out here acting a fool.

I greeted the men guarding the home before making my way through the house and into the backyard. To my surprise, it wasn't Uncle Enrique out here throwing a wild party, it was Papá. His elderly ass was sitting in his wheelchair while a woman young enough to be his granddaughter grinded into him with a string like bikini on. As I marched across the yard the girl pulled herself out of Papá's lap and bent over while shaking her ass. Papá leaned in and glided his tongue across her ass cheek before sipping on his Corona and locking eyes with me. I definitely wore an expression of disgust, that was some shit I could've gone the rest of my life without seeing.

"Papá, why have you been ignoring my calls?" I questioned once I was close enough for him to hear me.

The woman stopped dancing and sat down in Papá's lap. He finished off his Corona and waved the woman off before yelling into the backyard. "¡La fiesta terminó! (The party is over!)" At that moment it was some movie type shit, the music ceased and the women started to scatter. Uncle Enrique's bitch ass stumbled out of the sliding glass door with his left arm wrapped around a beautiful woman and a Corona in his left hand. By this time, I was fucking irritated. I spoke with Uncle Enrique before I booked the private jet and this nigga said that they weren't here. When Uncle Enrique's eyes landed on me, the look of guilt was evident. Then Uncle Macario stepped outside with Yaritza on his arm.

"Papá, ¿Por qué estás terminando la fiesta? (Why are you ending the party?)" Uncle Macario questioned, oblivious to me crashing the

LAKIA

party. He froze up at the sight of me and refocused his attention on Yaritza before sending her away. My presence told the story of a man who was enraged. Eyes full of fire, jaw tighter than a virgin's pussy, and fists clenched so tight that I felt my nails digging into the palms of my hand.

"Let's go into the house," Papá commanded, waving towards the sliding glass door.

Uncle Macario made his way inside and Enrique's bitch ass took off like the pussy he was. Upon entering Uncle Macario's office, I wasted no time digging into their asses.

"Y'all know y'all fucked up for the shit y'all pulled and that's why Uncle Enrique was lying saying y'all weren't answering the phone because you were out of the country on vacation and he wasn't sure where y'all went. I'm out here stressing and trying to protect my family while y'all are out here partying?"

"Don't take that tone with me, Alejandro. Yes, I ordered Alexander Senior and Junior to death. Imagine our surprise when we found the man who sold Priscilla the drugs that ended her life and he confessed that it wasn't even an accident and that your father got word to him to tamper with her cocaine and that he would be compensated generously! ¡Tu padre tiene que morir! (Your father has to pay!)" Papá roared but I wasn't backing down.

"That's not what happened! **I'm** the one who paid Mateo to do it. I had the message delivered under my father's name because I didn't want it to come back to me. Y'all know I barely fuck with my pops and if y'all would've found out and got back at him, it wouldn't have been a big deal to me but I never expected you to also go after my brother!" I lied effortlessly because I had plenty of time to mull over the perfect course of action during the flight over. Their faces stretched in shock and Papá grasped his chest. "Yeah, I did it. I was **desperate!** I came to you and asked for permission after Priscilla wouldn't give up the name of the man who shot **me**, *your grandson*, **twice...** in the chest!" I exploded, patting myself twice in the chest, right above my bullet wounds. "The drugs had a hold on her, I could've been **dead** that night. But y'all don't give a fuck about that huh? Yeah, Priscilla was family but what about *me*? Where is the *familial love* for **me**?"

"You know we love you, Alejandro!" Papá argued, his tone laced in concern.

"**Love** wouldn't have you asking me to forgive Priscilla for some shit that neither one of you would've forgiven her for. Papá, you would've shot her down like a dog if she gave some men your address!"

It was still a risk taking the blame for Priscilla's murder, knowing that I had nothing to do with her death, but I was willing to take that risk for my brother. This was the only way I could see us avoiding a war. They stood silently in shock, faces screwed up as they glared at me. Interrogation style questions floated around in my head as I waited for them to respond. *What if they saw through my lies? What if they still felt like I shouldn't have killed the powder head bitch? How the fuck is this shit about to end?* My nerves kicked in and I decided to lay out the rest of the facts behind my motives to kill my mother.

"Plus, Priscilla *kidnapped* my fiancée that you all claimed to love so much *and* she went to the Russo Mob and attempted to start a war between us because I put her in rehab after her kidnapping stunt. I suffered all of my childhood because of my mother's love for coke and dick. I didn't even want to enter the drug game, but Priscilla forced my hand because she spent all of the money my father left behind for me before I graduated from high school. She told my young impressionable ass that I had to be the man of the family and I believed her so I did what I had to do. The worst part of it all, I just found out that Priscilla was *fucking* the man who murdered Maceo... the *same* man that shot me," I ranted before tossing two cell phones on the desk. One belonged to Priscilla and the other belonged to Zack. Both phones were unlocked displaying pictures of Priscilla and Zack, probably high off of their asses, and Maceo's ring visibly present.

"Where is this mother fucker?" Uncle Macario roared, immediately making the connection.

"In the dirt!" I shot back, pulling Maceo's ring from my pocket. It was cleaned and I planned to keep it for myself because it was the only thing I had of my cousin but I passed it off to Uncle Macario. "I took care of him as soon as I got my hands on him, you know how I get down. If you weren't screening my calls, you would've known that. Now if you still feel like you want my brother's and father's heads after everything that I just laid out for you, then I guess you want a war with me too," I shrugged.

"You know I never wanted Priscilla to move to the US, I felt like she would get sucked up into some bullshit being so far away from our grasp. That's exactly what her ass wanted I guess. She loved the shopping and partying over there, I should've never let her go," Papá sighed. "If you felt that strongly about your mother and you say that's what you had to do, it had to be done. How is Yola? Grandson, I wish you would've come to me sooner," he uttered in a regretful tone.

Although I wanted to ask him why the fuck would I come to him after they didn't give a fuck about Priscilla playing a role in me getting shot, I was willing to overlook the bullshit. This was a common thing amongst elders in the family. They never wanted to be held accountable, apologize, or just recognize their bullshit.

"Yola is fine, she's solid, and I asked her to marry me," I grinned at the thought. "She's going to be my wife and I want to spend the rest of my life protecting her and keeping her happy. Since we are on that subject, I also wanted to let y'all know that I'm bowing out of the game now. It's never been where I wanted to be and now that I am where I want to be in life, I'm passing the shit off to my boy Vinny. He will be back on the third for me to make the introductions if you're willing to work with him as the head of my organization."

"Are you sure about this Dro?" Uncle Macario quizzed.

"Positive, plus Yola is likely pregnant. I just wanna focus on my legal businesses and continue to grow in that direction. Just know I won't ever turn into a weak motha fucka like Enrique," I laughed, lightening the mood.

"That's what you say now," Papá chuckled, taking a seat in Uncle Macario's chair. "Enrique has a good aim and used to be a young wild boy too but he got into pharmacy school and softened up. We will check back with you in a few years to see if you still got it in you. For now, we celebrate. Macario, go grab a bottle of champagne, it's a celebration. Love, life, and change."

"I'm with all that but pull out ya phone and call them hittas off my bro and Big Xan please," I pleaded and he complied without further argument.

We shared one glass of champagne that led to them restarting the party and my sucker for some authentic tacos ass stuck around for the party because Yaritza got in the kitchen and prepared some for me.

CHAPTER 20

Yola

Placing the twentieth call to Dro's phone and receiving the voicemail again had me sick to my stomach. Like the typical social media junkie, I plopped back down on the bed and scrolled through a few Instagram stories in an attempt to escape my reality. Allowing the stories to play out while I got into other people's business, I came across Yaritza's profile. There was my red headed devil clinking champagne glasses with his family in Mexico. He was having a blast while ignoring my damn calls and text messages. I was worried sick about him and he was out partying looking happy as hell. The fact that he was having a great time didn't bother me, it was his lack of communication and blatant disregard for my feelings that pissed me off. He could've told me that he was leaving, where he was going, or simply not ignored all of my calls or text messages. If the shoe was on the other foot he would be losing his fucking mind.

Enraged, I stormed around the room packing some of my shit into one of Dro's Louis Vuitton duffle bags. Honestly, I didn't need shit from out of here. I still had plenty of clothes and shoes at home but I wanted to make my point loud and clear when Dro's freckled face ass came home to see my shit gone. My emotions were all over the place with the way Dro was handling me. Since his ass got clingy, he claimed he couldn't spend a night away from me. Now he suggested that I was pregnant and went missing for the last twenty-four hours. Dro left this house without uttering a word and that made me feel like our bond wasn't as tight as I thought it was. Either way it goes, I was taking my black ass home. The hittas wanted Xan and Big Xan, not me.

Throwing the duffle bag across my shoulder, I stormed out of the door and passed the security guards that stood in front of the house. Our new babysitters were some official niggas, dressed in suits with ear pieces. I overheard Dro telling Xan that they were ex-military and that helped put my mind at ease when I was willing to be under their watchful eyes. Now that I was trying to take off, I prayed they wouldn't try to hold me hostage or no shit like that.

"We weren't notified that you needed to be transported to another location," Cameron, the shorter of the two men, voiced as I tossed the duffle bag into the backseat of my Lexus.

"I don't, I'm going by myself," I smiled.

I saw Benjamin, the other security guard, pull out his phone and speak into it. Cameron blocked my way and I rolled my eyes in frustration. A bitch couldn't even run off in peace. "I apologize Ms. Young, but I can't allow you to leave the premises without myself or Benjamin. If you'd prefer that Benjamin accompany you instead of me, we can switch posts for the day."

"No, I'd prefer that nobody accompany me… now get the fuck out of my way," I snapped.

The front door swung open and Xan stepped outside with Anya right on his heels. Huffing while stomping my feet slightly, I knew they were about to interfere with my plans. I had to lay in bed and listen to Anya get the life fucked out of her while I didn't know where the fuck Dro was and I wasn't about to do that shit again tonight. Granted, I didn't tell them what was going on, I sat my ass in the room and pouted while blowing Dro's phone up all night.

"Come on sis, why you trying to leave when you know everything going on around us," Xan grumbled. Before I could respond, a Toyota Corolla pulled up and a man stepped out looking just like Xan. He was an exact replica so it didn't take long for me to realize that this must've been their father Big Xan.

"What's going on out here?" He questioned like he even knew us.

Sighing, I cut my eyes back at Xan and Anya. "I'm leaving and I don't give a fuck what none of y'all have to say about…"

"Get Dro out here to calm her down," Big Xan commanded, cutting me off like he was about to run shit around here.

"That would be too much like right," I quipped, snapping my neck in his direction. "Unfortunately, we realized that I might be pregnant yesterday and Dro took off without a word to anyone and hasn't picked up his phone since."

"Oh Yola," Anya burst with excitement.

"Don't get happy because if this is how Dro is going to act, I'm done with his ass," I snatched my engagement ring off and tossed it in Cameron's direction. His reflexes kicked in and he moved to catch it, giving me just enough room to hop in my car. He pulled on my arm as Big Xan and Benjamin also rushed in my direction. Cameron tugged on my arm and wrapped an arm around my waist in an attempt to restrain me but Big Xan pushed his ass back.

"Don't be grabbing on her like that. Didn't you hear her say she might be pregnant?" Big Xan chastised him. I didn't know him from a can of paint but I appreciated the distraction and protective nature as I jumped in my car and sped off, all gas no brakes.

I could see Xan yelling at Big Xan, Benjamin, and Cameron in my rearview mirror but I had to get the fuck out of dodge before they got in their cars and chased my ass down. My heart didn't stop racing until I eased off of the gas and drove at a normal pace closer to the interstate. My phone was ringing off the hook with calls from Anya and I sent her ass to the voicemail every time.

Just when I had enough of my phone interrupting City Girls spit the lyrics to *Fuck Dat Nigga* and was about to block Anya's ass, a call came in from my mother. I debated for a moment on whether or not I should answer her call for fear that Anya and Xan called her to snitch like she was going to whoop me or something. Both of our mothers were under distant watchful eyes from some of Dro's men because they weren't feeling this situation at all. I let her call go to the voicemail and she immediately sent me a text saying that one of her co-workers needed a makeup artist. Deciding that I needed as much money as possible if me and Dro were really done, I called her ass back.

"Hello."

"Heyyyy, ma. Who needs a favor and did you let them know that I'm not cheap?"

"I already told them and she looked at your website and agreed to the prices. It's one of my co-workers from the bank, her daughter is getting married today and the makeup artist that she hired for her bridal party is pulling a *no call no show* and she's willing to pay anything to get you down there," she detailed.

"Okay, I'm already headed into the city. Text me the details and the woman's phone number and let her know I'm on the way and give her my information as well. Tell them a last minute job like this also comes with a three hundred dollar fee."

"I already let her know and they are cool. My co-worker's husband is a rich guy who owns a tech company. Get that money, baby," she cooed. "How have you been though? I've been trying not to worry like you said but that's easier said than done."

"I'm fine, ma, now let me go. I need to stop in a CVS or Walgreens to grab a few things to get this last minute job done."

"Okay Yola, I love you."

"I love you too," she replied and we ended the call.

When I stopped in CVS, I felt a few rapid cramps that made me stop to catch my breath. I knew what that meant so I tossed a pack of tampons into my basket. After checking out, I went to the bathroom and sure enough, my period came on. I wasn't disappointed at all either, it was Dro's know it all ass that put the bullshit pregnancy idea in my head anyways. Pulling out my phone, I opened up the app for my doctor's office and requested an appointment to get on birth control so I wouldn't have these problems in the future.

I was actually relieved because at the rate we were going, this money was going to be used on an abortion otherwise. Nigga wasn't going to switch up on me when I find out I was pregnant and expect me to take that shit. I was going to rid myself of that nigga and his baby. We didn't need a baby anyways, our relationship was still fresh and I was still trying to travel and enjoy life before bringing another life into this world. I'd hate to be as toxic as me and Dro could be with a baby added into the mix, no thank you. Since I knew the cramps would soon follow, I texted Daphne, the makeup artist that worked in my shop, to ask her if she wanted to split this money today. As always, she was down to double team this booking and get to the bag.

Thirty minutes later, I pulled up at Tabellas at Delaney Creek and was immediately ushered to the back of the venue where the bridal party was located. Daphne was already in the back working on one of the bridesmaids' faces when I arrived. I washed my hands and got to work too. There were six women in total, the bride and five bridesmaids. We worked hard and fast to get the ladies done in time for the ceremony to start. Since they were so behind schedule, the mother of the bride sent our payments plus a fat ass tip and insisted that we stay and enjoy the ceremony. I didn't have shit else to do and knew that they would probably find me at home anyways so me and Daphne grabbed a seat and joined the wedding guests for the ceremony and dinner. After indulging in the steak and lobster, I was extremely happy that we stayed. I spotted Teasha and Dontavius in the sea of people and rolled my eyes. I guess I wasn't too surprised to see them here, my mom did say her co-workers husband worked in tech just like Teasha and Dontavius so that was probably how they knew the bride and groom. Brushing the treacherous couple to the back of my mind, we got lost in the crowd of this three hundred person wedding and had a fucking ball like we knew these people.

CHAPTER 21

Dro

"Nigga, where the fuck you been?" Xan grumbled once I stepped across the threshold.

Mugging him, I didn't know what got into this nigga addressing me like he was fucking crazy. Prior to stepping through the door I felt invincible. My gift of gab was able to prevent a war that was sure to leave an immeasurable amount of bodies in the street. Of course there were a few lies told to my uncle and Papá, but Mateo was deceased so there wasn't anyone else to tell the truth besides Big Xan. I might not fuck with the nigga often but I knew he would take that secret to the grave.

"You might be doing too little too late," Big Xan's voice sounded off while coming down my hallway. I gave this nigga my address for emergency purposes only and his ass was over here looking a little too comfortable to me.

He was referring to the handful of gifts for Yola I entered the home with. I knew she was going to be pissed but I thought these gifts would make it up to her. My grimace morphed into a face of confusion because I didn't even know what that nigga was doing in my crib.

"What the fuck are you doing in my crib?" I addressed Big Xan before turning to Xan. "And why the fuck you sound like you got some stress on your chest? Matter of fact, I really don't give a fuck about any of that shit, I just want to let y'all know that they called the hit off. There is no longer a price on y'all heads so you two ugly motha fuckas can pack up and get the fuck out. I gotta go tend to Yola, I know she been poppin' shit because I broke my phone in Mexico and she was blowing my shit up."

"Where the hell have you been?" Anya's lil ass came rushing down the stairs with that cripple ass dog in her arm and Brownie running right behind her. I swiveled my head from side to side because she had to have been addressing Xan or Big Xan.

"I'm talking to yo block headed ass," Anya sassed.

"Yola! You better come get yo thin ass sister and her cripple ass dog," I yelled towards the second level.

"She isn't here! How dare you treat my sister like she didn't matter?" Anya fumed. Her little legs didn't stop moving until she was planted in front of me with her arms folded across her chest. The type of attitude that Anya presented was some shit I never saw her display before. "I am laxed about a lot of things but my sister isn't one of them."

"So y'all just let her leave?" I turned to Xan and Big Xan because now his earlier comment made sense.

"I sent Benjamin and Cameron to look for her," Xan informed me.

"That's fucked up, if it was Anya, I would've went to find her my damn self."

"I figured Yola would be alright because she isn't the one with a target on her back and you kept bragging about how much your people loved her when y'all went to Mexico. You the one who ran yo stupid ass off without saying shit to anyone. Plus they have the resources to actually find her, I don't."

"If something happens to my sister, I'm going to beat yo ass! I swear," Anya burst into a fit of tears. Releasing my grasp on the bags, I pulled Anya into my arms for a brief hug. "Chill, I am going to be able to find your sister and make shit right. Plus I squashed the beef with my other people so we straight, Xan and Big Xan are in the clear."

"For real?" Anya looked up at me with questioning eyes.

"For real, now let me grab my laptop so I can find your sister before she do some crazy shit we can't come back from," I advised them. Anya shoved Yola's engagement ring into my chest and I twisted my head to the side, clearly she was pissed for real. Darting towards the stairs, I took them two by two until I made it to the second level.

Logging into the app that tracked Yola's car, I saw she was at some type of event hall and wasted no time heading in that direction. Luckily, it was on the edge of Tampa and only twenty minutes away. When I pulled up to the spot, I breezed right past the people congregating near the entrance and followed the music until I found myself in the middle of a wedding party. A man stood in the middle of the floor with the microphone delivering a heartfelt speech that had everyone's attention. I scanned the crowd and didn't recognize a single face in the building. My first mind told me to yell Yola's name in the middle of this event to grab her attention but I was trying to respect the wedding party. Whipping out my phone, I opened the notes app and inserted a picture of me and Yola from our time in the Bahamas. She was so damn happy when we were down there and the smile was unforgettable. Then I added a message to the note as well before Airdropping it to the entire room.

The Note: Ion wanna fuck up these people reception but my girl is in here somewhere and she's mad as fuck at me. I'm trying to get back in her good graces without pissing her off further. Yola, I want you to know that I love you. I adore you. I would never do anything to hurt you. I fucked up by not communicating and moving the way that I did but I need you to stand yo fine ass up so we can go have a conversation like two adults. Yo pussy and your heart belongs to me so don't sit in here and play stupid. Love, Dro. P.S. If you're sitting next to Yola feel free to stand up and point her out so I don't have to wreck shit.

Moments later, the wedding guests' attention was refocused on their phones at random intervals then I heard the sweet sounds of Yola smacking her teeth with a loud huff a few feet away from me. She stood to her feet and stomped over to me, attitude present in the way she stomped over to me. Grinning, I met her in the middle of the wedding party. Now that I found my heart, I had a moment to observe the decor and setup at the wedding and it was dope as fuck.

"Why the fuck would you do that?" Yola grimaced, tugging on my arm as we headed away from the wedding.

"What? You wasn't answering the phone," I replied.

"You haven't answered your phone in over twenty-four hours so don't come at me with that bullshit. I was just returning the favor. But these are some nice church going people and you Airdropping a message about my pussy to the entire venue."

"Please," I waved that comment off. "Church folks fuck too. Shit, from all the kids they be having, they fuck raw a lot. You wasn't supposed to leave the crib anyways. What you doing way over here?"

"Stop questioning me like you didn't just fucking leave. You didn't say shit, you just left. Now you show your red headed step child ass up with all this bullshit," Yola retorted.

"I know I fucked up by not telling you what I planned to do but my mind was fucked up thinking about you and our family, I had to go handle shit. Plus I ain't used to consulting anyone before making decisions, I'm still getting used to that," I explained. "Now come home so I can show you all of the gifts I bought you."

"Okay and just so you know, I'm not pregnant, I got my period a few hours ago. You hopped up overreacting for no reason. I'm glad we had a slight scare though because I am going to get on birth control asap. The last thing you are about to do is take me out of the game when I'm just getting my shit together," Yola informed me.

"Damn," I grumbled because I knew for sure I missed my shot since she wasn't pregnant and was talking about birth control now.

"Yeah, so get all of those grand ideas out of your head," Yola quipped.

Leaning in, I kissed Yola deeply, praying that her attitude would subside. I missed her smart mouthed ass and was ready to go home and catch up on some sleep with Yola's thick frame in my arms. Since I thought she might be pregnant, my uncle and Papá wanted to celebrate and I indulged in the bullshit, even broke my phone in the process of partying with them wild motha fuckas. I had to stop in the Verizon store as soon as I touched down. When we broke the kiss, I locked eyes with the screamer I was fucking the day I met Yola. I hadn't conversed with her since that day, although she continued to call me until I changed my phone number on the night me and Yola decided to make shit official.

I was relieved that Yola's back was turned to her because she was staring a nigga down. Diverting my attention, I refocused on Yola and tried to usher her towards the exit but Teasha's dumb ass couldn't catch a hint.

"Dro!" She called out behind me and I was prepared to ignore her but Yola spun around. I didn't have to see her face to know that she was ready to spazz out.

Her eyes darted between me and Teasha before she spoke. "How you know *this* bitch?"

"Bitch?" Teasha puzzled until a sense of recognition washed over her face and her body tensed up.

"How you know this **bitch**, Dro?"

"I used to entertain her but I ain't seen her since the day you got me evicted from my apartment."

"***This*** the bitch you was fucking that day? I swear you used to stick your dick anywhere," she grumbled.

"All of the name calling isn't really necessary," Teasha protested.

"Teasha, you better move around before I beat yo ass for crossing my sister. Ion give a fuck that it was years ago."

Teasha's husband approached us from the side and I knew that this shit was about to go left when it didn't have to.

"What's going on Teasha, is everything okay?" Dontavius queried, placing his hand on the small of Teasha's back. Just my fucking luck, of all the places Yola could be, she was at the same wedding as these motha fuckas.

"Yes, everything..."

"No, everything isn't fine. Apparently, your friendly pussy wife was fucking him a few months ago before we met and now she is accosting him in the middle of this wedding like she isn't married to yo trifling ass. You two philandering mufuckas deserve each other," Yola rolled her eyes before Teasha could finish her statement.

"Alejandro, you fucked my wife?" Dontavius brushed past Teasha with rage filled eyes.

"I mean, she was throwing the pussy at me and basically stalking a nigga from the day y'all sold me King's," I shrugged, pushing Yola out of the way. "I'm not about to fight you over the hoe, as you can see, I'm happy where I'm at. Check that bitch."

"Oh no, not up in here." I kept my eyes trained on Dontavius with my hand gripped on my nine just in case he wanted to get stupid. His wife was a hoe and I'm sure that was a hard pill to swallow but it is what it is. In hindsight, I should've turned the bitch away when she came at me because I'd definitely spin any nigga block behind Yola. At that time, I didn't respect wedding vows because I never had feelings until Yola came along. It was too late to change that shit now anyways. If I was comprehending everything correctly, it sounded like Yola was insinuating that this was the nigga that left Anya for her best friend. If that was the case, I guess I was that nigga's karma because his wife was definitely obsessed before I changed my phone number.

"It's okay, Mrs. Miller, we are leaving right now. I'm sorry for the confusion in the back and I appreciate your business," Yola addressed the woman with a warm smile.

"You're welcome, sugar," Mrs. Miller smiled at Yola. She pulled me towards the exit but I wasn't the one to turn my back on the enemy so I was walking backwards. Dontavius and Teasha were engaged in a low argument but their body language said it all, that nigga was big mad.

"Get yo friendly dick ass in the car," Yola ordered, cutting her eyes at me once we were away from the party.

"Chill bae, I was fucking her when I was twenty-five. I turned twenty-six a few weeks before I met you. My prefrontal cortex wasn't fully developed," I laughed before planting a kiss on her lips and opening my truck door for her. "I drove here Dro, I need to get my car back home."

"Nah, I ain't letting you out of my sight, I'll get somebody to come grab your car. For now, we are going home, it's time to plan this wedding and get the rest of our life started."

CHAPTER 22

Anya
Six Months Later
February 14

Leave it to Dro and Yola to have a February wedding a few days before Valentine's Day. Of course their shit was over the top and Yola wanted everything perfect and Dro stood by her side, ensuring that all of her dreams came true for their big day. Now it was Valentine's Day and I scurried around the home that me and Xan shared decorating the entryway with red balloons and other romantic decorations.

Dro kept to his word and Xan ended up making him pay for a house to be built from the ground up on the opposite end of his property. Xan went with a five bedroom, four bathroom, four thousand square foot house that I absolutely adored. It was so close to Dro and Yola that I was still able to see my sister daily. Our houses were so close that we could either walk or drive the golf carts. If I wasn't busy with my own work I would sit with Yola at the shop and enjoy the company of the ladies. Xan remained in my home until he was able to move into his own house and naturally, I moved in with him. Now me and Yola were landlords because we rented our home out and life was drastically different from what it was a year ago.

Xan was at the office working on cases and I couldn't believe how far we came in all aspects of love and life. This was my first time having a Valentine in years. Yola and our moms always made sure I had flowers, chocolates, and other gifts on Valentine's Day but I was still alone at the end of the day. Our moms had their own husbands to entertain and Yola was usually getting spoiled by whatever man she was entertaining at the moment, this left me alone watching tv and eating ice cream alone.

LAKIA

I released the grip I had on the bouquet of red balloons and allowed the red strings to dangle in the entryway. Xan loved golfing so I purchased him a new set of Callaway Epic golf clubs and placed a huge red bow on top of them before leaning them up against the dining room table. There was a trail of red roses guiding the way from the dining room to the bedroom which was equally as decorated. I enjoyed every part of preparing for the day and decided that I might have to offer these services to the general public in the future.

With the decorations in place, I plopped down on the couch next to Brownie and Rex. They sat on the living room floor watching me the entire time I rushed about the house but they were too busy sharing their new Valentine's Day toys and treats to bother me. With my phone in hand, I watched a few TikTok videos of chefs preparing Chilean sea bass. I wanted to make the evening super romantic for Xan. Before I could finish the video, the Ring doorbell camera popped up on the tv screen and Yola's mug was staring at me. Sucking my teeth, I used my phone to unlock the door and she stumbled inside a few moments later.

"You really too lazy to open the door for a bitch?" Yola sassed, fighting her way through the balloons.

"Girl, what do you want? Shouldn't you be somewhere with your new husband? Getting ready for y'all honeymoon that starts tomorrow."

"Mind your business. It's only noon, the real events go down when the sun goes down," Yola bent over and started twerking. Frowning my face up, I shook my head at her before she continued. "Get up, I booked you a nail appointment at the shop for Valentine's Day. Just because you have a man this year doesn't mean we aren't going to do a little razzle dazzle. Let's go get pampered. You'll be home before Xan leaves the office," she assured me.

Glancing at my nails, I could use a fill in and wasn't going to refuse the free services. It was hard as hell to get an appointment with the nail techs in Yola's shop because they stayed booked. Rushing into my room, I grabbed a pair of sandals and the gift I bought for Yola before returning to the living room.

"Happy Valentine's Day!" I exclaimed, passing her the pink gift bag.

She grinned and plopped down on the couch to peek at her gift. "You got me two new Brandon Blackwood bags?!" She exclaimed and I loved watching her light up at the sight of a bag from her favorite purse designer.

"Okayyyyyy, Ms. Money Bags, thank you!" She exclaimed and I couldn't help the giggle that crept out.

My gifts were usually cheap and simple, a sentimental card, candy or something simple. This Valentine's Day was different, I got my marketing together and gained the confidence to charge what I was really worth. I was definitely entering my successful business era as an interior designer and I loved that for me. While Yola admired the bags, I kissed at the dogs and led them to their playroom. Brownie and Rex had an entire playroom setup for them to relax in when we weren't home. It contained two dog beds, a slide, and a plethora of toys that all overlooked the backyard. The backyard also had various items for the dogs to play with but we didn't leave them outside unless we knew we would be back within a reasonable time. Even in February, the weather was in the mid-eighties and our fur babies weren't built for that outside life.

Once the dogs were safely tucked away with water accessible, I rejoined Yola in the living room and we exited the home. As a wedding gift, Dro bought Yola a brand new black Porsche Cayenne with black and bordeaux red interior. This was my first time slipping inside and the car was impressive. The seats made you feel like you could just melt into them and I knew I would be adding a new car to my vision board.

When we made it to *Yo's Beauty Lounge*, I was ushered to my nail appointment and chose a pink and red for my nails today. While I got my nails done, I indulged in the free champagne that Yola always had on deck for her customers. By the time my nails were done I ingested more champagne than I intended and knew I probably shouldn't try to prepare the sea bass like I intended so I made a mental note to order food from Bonefish grill.

LAKIA

"Let's go grab some brunch from King's, I'm hungry," Yola requested as she watched Brianca rub cuticle oil on my finished nails.

"Dro opened up for brunch on a weekday?" I queried.

"Yeah, why you think I'm not sitting up under him right now?"

"I thought it was because you wanted to spend time with me. Thanks for letting me know how you really feel."

"Girl please, you know I love spending time with you," Yola smothered me with kisses along my cheek as I stood from my seat.

I giggled at her antics and washed my hands before we were on our way to our next stop of the day. Three months ago, Dro started opening King's for brunch on the weekends and special occasions. If I would've known they were open for brunch today, I would've texted Yola earlier to ask if she wanted to join me. I loved pasta but brunch food with a side of mimosas was a close runner up.

When we arrived at King's, Yola parked in her usual spot behind the building and we entered through the backdoor. I heard some classic Mary J Blige playing as I bit on my bottom lip in anticipation of the food. The chefs Dro hired for the weekends and special occasions to prepare brunch did their thing every time.

As we neared the end of the hallway that led to the main area of the club, I immediately realized what was going on. The DJ changed the song to *Propose* by Mary J Blige and I observed the red and white balloons filling the club. Only me, Xan, our parents, Yola, and Dro were in the club and my hand covered my mouth as the love of my life approached me dressed in a fitted button up and a pair of slacks. By his side were Rex and Brownie dressed for the occasion. Brownie wore a lilac dress and Rex wore a black vest with a matching lilac bow tie.

Tears welled up in my eyes as I grinned at Xan, floating across the club to meet him in the middle of the floor. Everyone who was important to me was in attendance and my stomach filled with butterflies as Xan kneeled while pulling a lilac ring box from his pocket.

"Anya," he started while licking his perfect brown lips. "From the moment I first saw you at the dog park, I couldn't keep my eyes off of you. That's partially the reason why Brownie was able to trample Rex that day, I was so busy stealing glances at you that I wasn't watching my dog properly," Xan expressed and I emitted a low chortle thinking back to that day I wanted nothing more than to beat his ass. "I was engrossed by your exterior beauty but your captivating presence drew me in and made me fall deeply in love with you. Your kind heart, intelligence, and the way you love those around you are the icing on the cake. You are my world and I will love you forever. Will you make me the happiest man in the universe and marry me?"

"Yes!" I exclaimed, leaning down to kiss Xan. Sucking his tongue into my mouth, I wished we were at home so I could do more than kiss him.

"Alright, alright!" Mr. Tom sounded off behind us.

"Relax, babe," My mom quieted her husband. Mr. Al was always the most overprotective of us so I was surprised that it was Mr. Tom with the outburst today.

"Nah for real, he ain't even slide the ring on her finger yet and we don't wanna see all of that," Mr. Al chimed in.

I chuckled as Xan slid the ring up my finger. Lifting the ring up to my face, I admired the oval lavender sapphire that was close enough to lilac for me. The sapphire was surrounded by diamonds with a rose gold band, exactly what I would've picked out for myself. With the ring secured on my finger, Xan stood to his feet.

"Ughhhh, I had all these grand plans to outdo you for our first Valentine's Day but I guess not," I exclaimed before jumping into his arms. Wrapping my legs around Xan's waist, I flung my arms across his shoulder and initiated one of those breathtaking kisses. Mr. Al was just going to have to look away because I was going to suck face with the love of my life until I couldn't anymore.

EPILOGUE

**Yola King
Over A Year Later
June 21st**

The lame ass traditional wedding music filled the distance while I sat in this uncomfortable ass wooden chair. Dro kept rubbing his frisky hands up my thigh and I had to swat that shit away. My ass cheeks were sore from sitting in this chair while they dealt with delay after delay. I loved Anya and Xan but this was some straight bullshit, they needed to get this shit over with so we could get from underneath this Florida sun. The Florida sun in June wasn't shit to play with and they had us sitting outside waiting for this wedding to start. They opted out of using a tent since this was supposed to be a quick ceremony but got damn it, they had a few minutes or I was grabbing Dro, getting in my golf cart, and heading home.

Yes, that's right, I said golf cart. After Xan continued his never ending hunt for a house, he decided he wanted to build one from the ground up. Dro owned so much of the land surrounding his home for privacy reasons that they agreed to build his home on the land. Now we lived within walking distance of each other but it was too hot to be walking between houses today.

"Why you being so fuckin' mean?" Dro questioned after I brushed his hand away.

"It's too fucking hot for you to be all over me, Dro," I snapped as Big Xan claimed his seat beside me.

All of our parents were in attendance and I loved the growth that took place between all of us. Dro and Xan were working on a relationship with Big Xan. I was a little worried at first because Dro and Xan were giving their father the blues but Big Xan was doing everything in his power to rebuild the tarnished relationship with his boys. Growing up without a father, I completely understood the void that Xan and Dro would never admit to so I always swooned over their budding familial relationship.

After being out of prison for a year, Xan hired his father to work as a paralegal at his law firm and it seemed to be working out quite well for the men. While Big Xan was in prison he spent a lot of time reading law books and even completed the course to become a paralegal. I loved going to Xan's law firm, a bunch of strong black men running a successful criminal defense law firm was a major accomplishment.

Big Xan passed me and Dro two small bottles of water before opening his to take a few swigs. My mom and Mrs. Anisha were seated across the aisle all booed up with their husbands while we were about to melt under the sun. I noticed Big Xan glance behind us where Mrs. Nadia and Mr. Phillip were seated and I'm not sure why the fuck he did that because his mood shifted immediately.

Then my girls, Hailey and Ralen, flew into town to join us for the occasion. To be honest, they just loved flying down to Florida and sulking up the sun so that's why they are here. Nonetheless, everyone who was important to me was in attendance today. I guzzled down some of the water and the music changed, signaling the start of the ceremony, and I dramatically whispered "thank the Lord" to myself because I was ready to go. I loved my sister and supported her in everything she did but this was some real bullshit right here.

Preme's tall lanky ass strutted down the aisle and it was no wonder his goofy ass was officiating this wedding. When I first met Preme, I thought he was an uptight, no nonsense type of man like Beast was. Every time I went to the law firm he was so serious, but getting to know him from our outings on the weekend where he brought his girl along, I quickly learned that he was just as silly as Dro and it made sense that they used to work together.

Once Preme reached the arch that was covered in white flowers I spotted my goofy ass friend Hailey strutting down the aisle in a white dress with emerald trim, tugging a red wagon that contained three rambunctious black and brown puppies.

"I swear to God them puppies ugly as a motha fucka," Dro whispered and I nudged him with my elbow.

They were ugly, but I still thought they were cute with their chocolate lab faces covered in black maltese fur. Apparently, Brownie and Rex were more than just roommates, they were clearly in love and Dro was right, the lab mixed with maltese combination was an extremely peculiar sight to see. They were puppies but already looked like they would take after Brownie and be bigger than their father's tiny ass. How they procreated was beyond me and something I don't even want to think about.

"It's fucked up though, I love, support, and cherish you. I don't hide our relationship like Rex hid his with Brownie, I love yo ass out loud and I can't get a jit," Dro continued talking shit in my ear.

"Boy, I already told yo begging ass when we are thirty, we can start having kids. We have the rest of our life for that, we still have goals to accomplish and you are in the process of putting together your second car show this year, the last thing you need is a baby," I lectured him for like the hundredth time before leaning over to plant a kiss on his perfect pink lips. Cupping his cheeks, I stared into his handsome freckled face. "I love you and we are going to have as many babies as we want once we are in our thirties."

I refocused my attention on the aisle as Xan exited the back of their home and swaggered down the aisle with Brownie in toe. She was dressed in a cream dress with a huge emerald bow on her back. Now that the ceremony was underway and I was more relaxed, I admired the ambiance that was carried out in the backyard. All of the flowers were white and emerald, matching the bow on Brownie's dress. With the leash grasped tightly in his hand, Xan claimed his spot in front of Preme. Next, Anya walked down the aisle with Rex by her side. He was dressed in a full black tux with an emerald green bowtie. Shaking my head, I thought about how much Rex grew since Anya bought his little ass home. Once Anya reached the arch, the music stopped and Preme started the ceremony.

"Alright, it's hot and Anya and Xan were taking forever trying to dress all these mutts," Preme fake coughed, causing me and Dro to laugh. "I mean dress all of these dogs."

"Just say the lines Preme," Xan shook his head.

"My bad bro, I'm getting to it. We are here to bless the union between Rex and Brownie in holy dog matrimony. We bless Brownie and Rex in the name of joy, fertility..."

"Fertilityyyyyy!" Dro blurted out. "Ain't no way y'all want them to have another litter of ugly ass dog jits."

"Man shut up," Xan laughed.

"I'm just reading the lines Anya wrote for me," Preme defended himself with a smile and his hands raised in surrender.

"It's what I saw on a website called HuffPost. Just finish the lines," Anya giggled.

"Okay," Preme cleared his throat before continuing. "May these pups never go hungry and always be filled with love! Now Rex, do you take Brownie to be your wife?"

Anya placed her palm in front of Rex and he hopped up on his back legs and placed his right paw in her hand. Preme repeated the line for Brownie and she placed her paw in Anya's hand as well.

"By the lil power invested in me, I now pronounce you pups dangerously in love and recommend that your parents get one of you neutered to avoid another ummmm... unique litter of puppies. Arf! Arf!"

Big Xan stood and passed Xan a long dog treat which he then placed on the ground in front of the dogs for them to share. The dogs went crazy fighting for it and I watched in amusement thinking about how they had us waiting in the hot sun for this. One thing about Xan and Anya, they were extra as fuck about their dogs and I couldn't wait to see them as parents. Their kids were going to be spoiled to no end. Hailey pulled the puppies from the wagon and they rushed over fighting for some of the dog treats too.

"There are refreshments inside for us and Ralen, you can let your dog play with them. They have access to a water fountain in the back and plenty of dog treat buckets are placed around the yard," Anya explained to the wedding guests.

Their backyard was pretty much an oasis for the dogs with a pool in the middle. I'd never get in their pool either because I'm sure the dogs hop in there any time they feel like it. Won't have fur in my coochie giving me BV. Dro kept his face down there too much for all of that. "Come on, it's hot," I complained, gripping Dro's hand.

We went into the home and I promise the air conditioner never hit as good as it did today. If it were anyone else asking me to attend a dog wedding in the middle of summer, I would've immediately declined but it was Anya and I loved her so we were there. I'm positive that Dro shared my sentiments when it came to Xan and Brownie. After washing my hands, I retrieved a bottle of champagne and poured enough glasses to spread around. There were only eleven people in attendance so the process was swift.

Raising my champagne glass in the air I decided to propose a toast. "This is a shoutout to everyone in this room. I love you all dearly and I wish nothing but the best for us this summer. Ladies get ready to act real baaaaaaaaad! Vegas, LA, and Jamaica are all on our travel line up." I exclaimed before tapping the glasses together. Everyone sipped from their glass except for Anya, and Xan sneakily removed hers and I didn't miss that exchange at all. "Anya, you didn't," I gasped and a huge grin spread across Xan's face.

"What?" My mom questioned, sipping from her glass.

"We were hoping to wait until after the first trimester to make an official announcement but since our parents are here, we are expecting a baby," Xan grinned, placing a protective hand over Anya's stomach.

"You ruined our hot girl summer itinerary because you don't know how to hop off the dick fast enough!" I whined, really in my feelings for real.

"Aye aye aye!" Mr. Al waved his hand in the air. "We don't wanna hear all of that."

"At all, please act like your parents are in the room," Mr. Tom chimed in.

Big Xan dapped Xan up and they shared a celebratory hug. That's probably the first time I noticed Big Xan smile since he saw Mrs. Nadia and Mr. Phillip all hugged up earlier. He was usually in good spirits but even a blind man could see how his mood switched drastically when Mrs. Nadia and Mr. Phillip were around. He wanted that old thing back, but as the saying goes, "when one man fucks up, another man lucks up." I made a mental note to see if I knew anybody with a fine ass single mama that I could hook Big Xan up with, he needed to get over Mrs. Nadia because she was deeply in love and that was clear.

While I was deep in thought about my ruined summer plans and playing matchmaker between a few fifty year olds, Dro talked even more shit in my ear. "We been together longer than them, they just got married in the courthouse two months ago and they acted like they were scared of each other for so long but they having a jit before us. Cold world."

"Boy," I snickered, turned to face Dro, and wrapped my arms across his shoulder. "You know random sex all around the house at any time of the day will no longer be a thing once we have kids right?"

"Damn, you right," he cupped my ass with his big hands and tapped it gently, but I wanted more than he was offering as that sensation sent a tingle down my spine that somehow ended in my yoni. "Come on, let me bend you over something in the house so the ache in my heart will disappear."

Smirking at my husband, I gripped his hand and slipped out of the house while all of the attention was on Xan and Anya. "Aunty and uncle sound so much better than mommy and daddy now that you put it into those terms," Dro mentioned once we were outside. He slapped my ass super hard without warning and I emitted a low moan. Dro knew that was the key to get me to submit to anything he wanted, he handled me so roughly but with care and I loved it. I swear the best thing I ever did was fall in love with the nasty ass plug next door.

THE END

Make sure you join my Facebook group: https://www.facebook.com/groups/keesbookbees
Mailing list: https://bit.ly/2RTP3EV

FOLLOW ME ON SOCIAL MEDIA

Instagram: https://instagram.com/authorlakia
Facebook: https://www.facebook.com/AuthorLakia
Facebook: https://www.facebook.com/kiab90
TikTok: https://www.tiktok.com/@authorlakia

Join me in my Facebook group for giveaways, book discussions and a few laughs and gags! Maybe a few sneak peeks in the future.
https://www.facebook.com/groups/keesbookbees
Or search Kee's Book Bees

ALSO BY AUTHOR LAKIA

Surviving A Dope Boy: A Hood Love Story (1-3)

When A Savage Is After Your Heart: An Urban Standalone

When A Savage Wants Your Heart: An Urban Standalone

Trapped In A Hood Love Affair (1-2)

Tales From The Hood: Tampa Edition

The Street Legend Who Stole My Heart

My Christmas Bae In Tampa

The Wife of a Miami Boy (1-2)

Fallin For A Gold Mouth Boss

Married To A Gold Mouth Boss

Summertime With A Tampa Thug

From Bae To Wifey (1-2)

Wifed Up By A Miami Millionaire

A Boss For The Holidays: Titus & Burgundy

Miami Hood Dreams (1-2)

A Week With A Kingpin

Something About His Love

Craving A Rich Thug (1-3)

Risking It All For A Rich Thug

Summertime With A Kingpin

Enticed By A Down South Boss

A Gangsta And His Girl (1-2)

Soul Of My Soul 1-2

Wrapped Up With A Kingpin For The Holidays

New Year, New Plug

Caught Up In A Hitta's World

The Rise Of A Gold Mouth Boss

A Cold Summer With My Hitta

Soul Of Fire

Sweet Licks (1-3)

Riding The Storm With A Street King

Running Off On My Baby Daddy At Christmas Time

Made in the USA
Columbia, SC
06 March 2024